The Darkened Path

Lora Wilder

Contents

1. Chapter 1 ... 1

2. Chapter 2 ... 16

3. Chapter 3 ... 24

4. Chapter 4 ... 38

5. Chapter 5 ... 47

6. Chapter 6 ... 55

7. Chapter 7 ... 67

8. Chapter 8 ... 79

9. Chapter 9 ... 90

10. Chapter 10 ... 102

11. Chapter 11 ... 110

12. Chapter 12 ... 123

13. Chapter 13 ... 133

14. Chapter 14   143

15. Chapter 15   153

16. Chapter 16   162

17. Chapter 17   174

18. Chapter 18   188

19. Chapter 19   202

20. Epilogue   214

Chapter 1

Three Months Earlier

They're coming. A whisper echoes in my skull. Their words pull me into a trance of darkness. My mind pulls away from me and fills with their voices. They cast me into a spell. Help us.

"Serelia." A faint voice begins to drown out the rest. "Come on. Snap out of it." A clicking rings in my head.

"You're missing the damn movie, girl. Pay attention!" While I try to regain my surroundings, there's a flick of something on my face and a dampness on my cheek.

My eyebrows scrunch as I become more alert, a loud screaming blares from the television replacing their whispers. With my eyes still in a blur, my hand raises up and picks off an object resting on my cheek. "Did you throw popcorn at my face?" My words catch in my throat, tossing them out as a murmur.

Rising upward on the sofa into a sitting position, I twist my head to the person beside me. A dim light from the television shines against my best friend, Levana, as she takes a bite of pizza while trying to shake me out of my dry-spell.

"You did it again, and during the best scene too. I had no choice," she teases while proceeding to toss another piece of popcorn towards me as though she was feeding pigeons in a park.

"You know it's not polite to play with food." I pick a fry off the tray table in front of us. Salt and grease salivate my mouth as I chew on the crunchy treat.

"Again, you dozed off when this movie was finally starting to get good. I wouldn't be who I am if I let you miss it," she taunts me, taking another bite of her pizza.

"I'm sorry," I grin. "My brain must've malfunctioned from all of the calories we've eaten. You brought more food than ever this time." My eyes move toward the dining and tray tables placed around the living room. Plates of burgers, fries, pizza, chips, and any other snack imaginable scattered around. The grease of it all wafts up my nose and my mouth waters.

Moments like this with Levana are some of the few that remind me I am a teenager. That there is a possibility of normality for me. It's always been so easy with us, from the first time she brought food to my door and everyday since.

She was there when it all became too much, holding a bag of cheeseburgers and a movie disk. After that, it became our tradition. I always laugh at the visual of Levana slinging a bulging bag of food over her shoulder every Saturday.

Levana saved me.

She has been the only person to stand by me. I have missed days of school when I could no longer tolerate the jokes and laughter. Hearing the mumblings of the incident. A wildfire of rumors spread. My trauma was twisted in ways to entertain the average teenager.

"You were mumbling something this time—rudely interrupting the movie—might I add. What were you thinking about?" She asks as her eyes focus on the screen.

I hesitate. No one else can know; if they knew about the whispers, they would run. Label me the lunatic who cried wolf.

The years that followed the accident left the trace of the wolves, stalking me with each step. Keeping me alive in a physical sense, but dead in every other. Every moment is filled with overwhelming emptiness I could have forgotten how to breathe and not cared.

I've plastered on a smile and played by each day as it goes. Pretending everything is okay, that everything is sane.

In this instance, pretending that I'm too focused on the food in front of us and trying to figure out which to eat first.

"Earth to Serelia." Levana waves her hand in front of my face. "I'm right here, clearly talking. You can't ignore me. Food rots your brain, you know." My grin grows wider and I shake my head.

"The saying is 'TV rots your brains,' not food, dummy." I tease before sticking my tongue out.

"Whatever, you know what I'm saying." She chuckles before turning back to the screen. After the credits roll, Levana slips in the second movie, the RedBox case revealing a romantic comedy.

Hours of delightful peace pass before a buzzing vibrates from Levana's phone, the screen lights up with a message notification. Her smile drops when she scans the phone, repeating her mother's text telling her to go home. When she leaves, it's about five in the afternoon; a wave of tiredness washes over me, and I head upstairs to my room.

My feet drag up each step. My body is so tired that a simple staircase is an insurmountable climb, becoming a tall mountain. I move to the washroom in hopes that a splash of cold water will pry the tiredness away. My head tilts up, where my eyes peer at the glass in front of me, studying a face I no longer recognize.

From my dark mahogany hair, frizzed and messy, to the haunting of my 'freaky' jade-green eyes peer into my soul, judging the being looking back, telling me this isn't who I am supposed to be.

It's difficult to look at my own reflection, to see a stranger in the place where my face used to be. I peer at the image of my mother sitting inside one of the boxes—an old polaroid outlined by a wooden oak frame. A forsaken memory of when we laughed and played, the innocence of having fun on the grass in front of our house. After that, all the bad moments that followed this moment flood in like an avalanche.

I attempt to find the little girl from the picture, the one who laughed, who was genuinely happy. A girl who had a face that showed no worries, that had gapped teeth and dimples highlighting her smiling cheeks. How I would warn her of what will become of her life soon enough, if I could have been better prepared for the trauma. Though, can anyone truly prepare for the end of the world they know?

I was young- too young to understand the cruel realities that life held. Sometimes, I wish I could forget everything that happened. That I could live in a blissful ignorance like the rest of society, yet my memories sink into my skin with sharp claws.

Noting every detail of the picture, from her constant smile and her hopeful eyes, I try to search for any hint of resemblance between my mother and I. That's all people would say when I was a child, how similar she and I looked, and still I've never been able to understand what they saw. To me, my mom and I were complete opposites.

My mother always had a natural beauty, confident no matter how she appeared to the world, unlike me who drowns in insecurity. She was youthful and lively in the eyes of society, perfect inside and out to the world. At least, before her insanity revealed itself.

Boxes litter the ground, filled with items from what is left of my innocence. Packed, ready to be donated or moved to the next place I'll live at. Perks of being an underaged orphan, or so that's what child services call me.

Even though my mother isn't dead, she is in the eyes of the court. It's not like I have any polaroids with my father. Instead, they pawned me off to my grandmother, who truly had no problem taking me in with her saint-like heart. She moved into this house with me when my mother was taken away, figuring I needed at least one piece of stability. Now she thinks it's time for us to leave here and move into her home hours away from here.

Change has always been the worst of my enemies, that and the illness that has followed me for nine hundred and seventy days. Glaring back at my reflection, I try to find any hint of recognition of the face looking back.

Apprehension and repressed dejection cloud my mind and have left no concerns for my ghoulish appearance. My eyes are almost non-existent, hiding behind darkened bags that sink deep into the sockets. Tangled hair covering a majority of my face behind the frizz. My natural-tan skin now discolored from lack of sun, the same gray of a rotting corpse, along with my lips peeling and cracking from dehydration.

They say you need to survive in order to truly find yourself. I've already survived enough, I'm trying to figure out what I'm living for. Practicing my smile for the world, I try to mimic my mother in our picture, hoping my acting skills are so good that not one person asks if I'm okay. I always dread those questions, all the Are you okay and How are you feeling today?

Our accident happened a few years ago, but the depression and nightmares have never gone away. My mother almost killed me because of a mental breakdown. How the fuck are you supposed to get over that? The nightmares feel so real, as if I actually lived it; but I did, didn't I?

They'll never understand me, and how I feel like I belong in a padded cell alongside my mother. They don't realize how desperately I wish to trade places with them, no matter who they are. To have even an idea of a white picket fence life and sense of normality. Though, I never say any of that and give the scripted phrase, "I'm fine, thank you for asking," with a smile wider than Cheshire Cat's.

I don't realize how my knuckles squeeze the granite, pressing down so forcefully they turn snow white. A pang slices in my heart, loneliness burying me alive.

A broken sound comes from deep within. I bite my tongue, and blood rushes in my mouth. Broken. My soul was shattered when we had our accident. My heart turned to glass when she was taken away. My brain numbed as I realized what would come to my life afterwards. Even my body crumbles everyday, like a glass doll who was dropped too many times. I'm broken.

After a few minutes, I calm down enough to halt my tears, and clear my mind for a moment. My hand moves towards the faucet, twisting the sink's knob to release steaming, hot water. It hits my palms as I cup my hands and bring them to my face, wiping away any indication of sorrow.

When I wipe my eyes, a shadow flickers behind me, a small figure running. Common sense tells me it is a trick of my eyes, but still, I turn around and sidle into my bedroom. The figure runs in front of me again and I realize it's not a hallucination, but rather a flash of a memory. A projection of my childhood being played like a movie.

A counting of numbers rings inside my head, the voice of my mother sounding out as she reaches ten and shouts "ready or not here I come." I twist my head and a younger version of me hides behind a structure of plush animals, stacked up tall enough to cover the entirety of my four year old body. My mother sneaks into my bedroom, a mischievous smile on her face.

"I found you!" My mother's voice squeals as she carries me up, my eager screams filling the room. Laughter takes over, so loud you'd think there were thirty people instead of two. How can a loving mother and a happy young girl turn into the people we are today, insane and scarred? How that laughter will die in a few years and like this movie of memories, this dream will come to an end.

My breath quickens as I relive my memories before they start to fade. Get out. Adrenaline rushes through my veins and a sudden burst of energy helps me run out into the street, running as fast as my legs will allow. I need to get out of this house, and more importantly, the memories trapped inside of it.

My feet become my guide, moving without direction, far away from my house. As it disappears from my view, I start to gather my surroundings, which isn't so hard considering the compact size of our town. A flock of people surround me as I snake between stores and houses.

Passing by one diner, a family of four sits at a table. The parents watch their children with bright smiles as they enjoy a meal. There's a group of people in front of a house barbecue, a jumper is filled with laughing children and music blares from their speakers. I pass by the town's park, children running wild, adults catching up with their friends, teens my age socializing. All these people live their lives so effortlessly, so gleefully.

Through the trees and grass, I end up in between the edge of the park and a small wooded area. The trees stand tall above me and I'm stuck between an unfamiliar woods area that probably stretches on for miles, and the town behind me that has brought me nothing but grief.

Maybe I should run deeper into the woods, leave the town and see how far my legs will take me. Perhaps one day finding someplace I can start fresh and create a new identity. Start completely over and give myself a chance for happiness that I know I'll never find here. Or even end up at the edge of the world if such a thing were to exist. If these woods go out far enough, I'll find myself overlooking a cliff, and all of space and time will be frozen.

I can just jump.

The sound of something jostling near me snaps me out of my thoughts—a figure moves behind one of the far off trees in front of me. Squinting to try and get a better view, I watch the trees to see if there is something actually there, or if I'm losing my mind. A rustle sounds in the distance and there it is again, a quick and sudden movement jostling behind the trees.

"Hello?" This is how people end up in murder movies, Serelia. What do you expect, some random person to come out and start a friendly conversation?

Curiosity fills my being. Only seconds pass before impatience beckons me and I take a step forward. Then another one. My body shivers the closer I move to the tree, focusing all my senses onto it. A subdued snarl fills the air, quiet but guttural, holding so much weight it could send this town crumpling to the ground. A whimper tickles my throat as I creep closer, the growling reverberating louder. Realization hits- all the whispers are gone. Dead silent, waiting to see what I do next. In a moment that draws on forever, I can feel the tree's bark scratch the palm of my hand, the growl shushing without fade.

Before I'm able to peer fully around the wide tree, a whisper yells in my brain. A voice, different from my own, warning me. Leave. Don't let them catch you. As the voice echoes, a crackle sounds from the opposite end of the tree, whatever is behind getting ready to pounce. Like a switch, common sense catches up to me, whirling my body around and shoving me into a run. Without hesitation, I hustle through the woods, the only noise coming from my feet hitting the leaf-covered dirt and the heavy panting of my breath, each inhale burning my lungs.

A strain pulses through my legs as I sprint, running from the darkness. My feet behave as if they gain a mind of their own, lunging my body forward with no end in sight. The daunting woods loom around.

As the park comes back into view, the treeline greets me like an old-friend, and there's a second pair of footsteps nearing me. A rapid sound of feet thumping the ground, sticks and leaves being snapped beneath. If I turn around or pause for even a second, whatever is behind me will strike. I'll be dead. Pumping my arms and forcing my legs to continue on, I push forward, my fight or flight kicking in. This thing behind me is out for blood—my blood.

Coming closer to the light, to the laughter-filled park, a small sense of hope sparks in me. Though, like air to a flame, it blows out instantaneously. My foot gets caught on a tree branch, tossing me forward and I land on a patch of hard dirt, my arms reactively moving in front of me.

A conglomeration of curse words escape my lips, my ankle feeling like it snapped off my leg and if I were to look back it would be dismembered from my body, stuck on that stupid branch behind me.

Panic sends my heart beating like a machine on overdrive, ready to malfunction and burst through my chest. I'll become a doll being torn apart. Every step closer, every hot breath against my skin, is a second closer to my demise. One where the only thing left will be crimson-stained dirt and leaves, blood dripping from ivory teeth of any animal that feasts on my remains.

A numbness spreads through my legs, casting out the pain of my fall, preventing me from escaping. Tremors shoot up my arms, unable to hold myself up any longer, to fight back in any way.

Blood clashes with the sweat, my lungs drown with air that is trapped inside, words fail me. Not even a whimper. Anxiety floods, my eyelids press together, as I wait for my inevitable death. I begin to count.

Like the game my mother and I used to play, numbers reverberate in my mind. Each step the monster draws nearer, another second passes. By the time I reach ten, perhaps peace will be revived. I'll end up in a place of fun and games, innocence and isolation. Maybe in the clouds, or along the ocean's waves. Sand and water surrounding instead of dirt and trees. The possibility that death is in fact better than life, or at least this life.

In six seconds, I will have my freedom come. Release of all the questions and comments, telling me to get over this unending sadness.

In five, I will feel no more pain. No more being an outcast or disgrace to this world.

Four, the scars will disappear and tears will dry. The accident will become a memory that will no longer haunt me. The whispers will fade and I'll have nothing but serenity.

Three...

Two...

One...

Silence.

The clock ticks no more. Its hot breath grows cold, and all footsteps cease behind. Yet I am still alive.

My eyes flutter open, still expecting to see a baleful beast inches away. Death is still coming, and there's still hope for an everlasting peace. A reaper here to take me to my final resting place. An angel to fly me to the heavens above. The right release of pressure from my eyelids casts a blur of browns and greens meshed together. But that doesn't stop me from seeing it... them.

What lies near is something much darker than any heaven or hell.

My sight trains on a shadow in the clearing ahead. Colors blended turn into shapes, which turn into objects, yet the shadow's the same.

You're not safe. To tell the difference between my thoughts and the whispers grows difficult, perhaps they're the same. Who's to say otherwise at this point?

Gazing upon the figure, I realize this is what was chasing me. The reality lands like a punch to my gut. It has to be. But why would they stop? Why not kill me now? Maybe it's waiting for me to run, finding more enjoyment in the sport of killing. The game of cat and mouse, they want me to suffer as I die, knowing I couldn't outrun them.

He's here. The words repeat, clearer this time, as if they parted from my own lips. The fact that my mouth is sealed shut, my teeth gritting against each other, is the only indication that they didn't.

His veiled figure stands a distance away, taunting me to join him. The whispers of the wolves turn to white noise and his voice speaks above the rest. A soft but heavy whisper speaks, "You."

"Who are you?" I yell, my voice cracking with each word, curiosity creating a tingling sensation in my bones.

"Serelia." His voice rings out and his silhouette draws closer. His presence, his warmth, nears, and familiarity overpowers curiosity. He doesn't seem real, more of a memory than an actual being.

He's waiting for me, his being calling to me. Though I can't see his face, his watchful eyes signal me closer. I need to go to him, to identify him. His whisper reverberates around the silence, his body approaches.

"Find me."

The more he nears, the darker the scene becomes. Somehow his figure grows smaller, but I know he's only a matter of feet from me now. My breath quickens as I anticipate him reaching me. My eyes strain on his figure, one that doesn't appear human. Before I can grasp what is occurring, the figure finally comes face to face with me and I can see him clear as day in this darkness. The him isn't a man.

It's a wolf.

Chapter 2

My trembling hand finds itself pressed against my parted lips, a gasp warming my shaking palms. The rest of my body remains paralyzed, frozen in fear as I face the creature that stands only feet away. It's blood-red eye highlighting against the other shaded black marble. A mix of salt and pepper fur illuminates the darkened forest. My heart races, readying itself to possibly stop. Even with the realization that I might die, a part of me can't help but notice how beautiful this creature is before me.

A wave of dizziness crashes into me like water against a cliff. My knees struggle to hold their balance. Fear pools through me, a warm tide washes through my veins. Eerie silence is deafening.

The wolf fades into darkness, yet his presence remains.

Then, a person descends from where the wolf vanished—waiting in the shadows. Four legs become two, a wolf transforms into a human. He remains there, a statue in the distance. Fear turns to confusion, the trembles of my body cease.

Recognition brews inside me, the sense of security drawing me to the darkened figure. Something about him brings feelings of home. He emerges, shadowing me like a small building. Hazel eyes shine against a face that knows no emotion. His expression is that of a ghost, still, his warmth reaches me from where he stands.

Aside from a darkened presence, he looks like any other ordinary being. A jacket hugs a muscular body, the scent of leather battling the damp leaves and pine. Haughty, broad shoulders carry an aura of somber authority that runs down to taut hands hanging at his sides. A stance so firm, he could be a soldier in a lineup. A charming impression clashes with intimidation, as if a white knight had an affair with the devil. Is it really possible he was a wolf only moments ago?

Above all, familiarity sprouts within, stirring inside though I can't place where. No name clicks inside my mind, even his face is one I've never seen. His presence, though, wreaks of remembrance and something in my head is blocking it from emerging.

His eyes—a blank, but penetrating, stare that can pierce any soul. They shout to me, urging me to remember—to trust.

After an eternity of silence, his voice breaks the air. "Serelia... come home. They're coming." His broken sentences echo, a seriousness expressed through a deepened voice that clashes like a distant thunder. A surge of alarm chills my spine when he speaks, his message unnerving, but his manner calm.

I can only bring a single word to leave my mouth. "What?" Even alone, my voice quivers, the curve of my lips quaver with the simple question. A part of me tries to remember this isn't real, it's impossible. Yet somehow it also feels like the only true thing that has happened in weeks. All my fear drains inside me, questions replacing it. Even with my uneasy response, the boy continues unfazed, his empty expression never changing. "Where's home?" This time, my question sounds with great clarity, still, there's a shakiness as I attempt to manage each word.

With no answer, he turns away from me and saunters into the shadows once more. My lips part, a need for him to return and acknowledge me. "Wait," I clamor towards the darkness, but he was gone before my words could reach him.

Common sense warns me to stay put, that the last thing I need to do is chase a boy on a hurt leg in these harrowing woods. My conscience reminds me that this is insanity brewing fantastic delusions, to pick myself up and go home. Leave these woods and let it become a bad memory that vanishes in time.

Instead, I drown out the subconscious and any other opposing thoughts. "Follow him," I whisper to myself, forcing my body to ignore my mind. "Just go," and with that, I spring into motion, racing to the shadows. The prey chasing the predator, the hunted now chasing the hunter.

I barely move a few feet until his figure appears ahead. Before he is fully absorbed by darkness, he halts in his trails and I continue to near, playing a game of chess, trying to be the quickest to advance. His back still faces me as I come only feet a few years away.

"Don't follow," his instruction sounds in a whisper. Even standing in a distance, his words sound as if he's beside me, speaking into my ear-in my head. "You will know when your time comes. Beware of those who are in your life; they are not who you believe them to be. Find a way to save yourself. Once you understand how, come and save us."

My feet come to a dead halt in the midst of my tracks. A throbbing pressure forces inside my head, like two brains are fighting for control inside my skull. Like he's inside my head.

Even though he speaks in simple phrases, clear words to ensure understanding, I'm unable to process a single thing he said. Why am I not safe? Save who? Who can't I trust? I don't even have the opportunity to ask for he proceeds to walk away without another word.

This time, I don't chase after him.

In a matter of steps, darkness swallows him and I'm left here, all alone with whispers and pains of my body as my only companions. My mind racks around each word, picking apart every letter he uttered, trying anything to understand even part of what he meant. Words become lost to me at a stand still, while my mind runs in circles, looking to escape the tedious trails of round and around.

After his presence departs, my senses collectively shout a giant, screw it, to his orders and leaps into motion. Pushing forward, my mind refuses to be left without a wider collection of questions than I had from before entering these woods. I need to find him. To know what he means. I know he wants to say more, he has to. As my heart jets, my stomach churns with a roller coaster of nerves and doubts.

With a few steps deeper into the unfaltering woods, hope dawns through my legs as they slow. My feet stand in the same place he was only seconds ago, his tracks outlined in the dirt. In the darkest parts between the trees, a faint light gliders down to me. A spotlight shining on the worst play in history, and I'm still trying to figure out my role.

One question bellows louder than the others, incapable of being ignored. It replays again and again in my head above all the whispers: is this all just a dream? For the truth of this being reality is too unfathomable for even the most fantastic dreams. His voice is still in my head and all I hear are those two simple words. 'Come home.'

As the broken record of my brain repeats, a flash of a face appears— someone new. A vision unveiling like a lightning strike, yet his eyes were crystal clear. Or rather a forest green, similar to mine. The illusion disappears, but his eyes, his sad eyes, remain. Another pull of familiarity drives within, even though his image appeared for a brief moment, it stays with me. As if I could draw his facial structure by that simple memory, and somehow I know that he is watching me, protecting me.

Who are these people? What do they mean to me? What do I mean to them?

With a heavy heart I realize there is only one person who can answer these questions for me.

"Serelia?" Unable to comprehend a voice, my breath halts and the hairs of my eyebrows brush together, questions surging if he returned, or ever left.

"Are you okay?" Relief eases through me for a moment, only a moment, as the voice processes and recognition swallows me. After that second, a faint-lasting tranquility turns to anger, and I whip my head around only to lock eyes with a familiar face. In the next second, regret fills, weighing on my heart.

I'd rather be eaten by the wolves.

Memories of betrayal return. How I could go the rest of my life without seeing his face, but yet, here he stands.

"What do you want, Finn?" My words pinch with a sharp snap, I turn my gaze down to break eye-contact.

"No need for hostility, Ser. We're still best friends." His whispered breath pauses, there's a small hesitation in his hands, nearly reaching for me, but when my eyes draw back to him, he pulls away.

"Correction," venom spit with each letter. "We were best friends, past tense. Doesn't mean anything now. Just go."

"I saw you running out here and that you tripped on that branch. I called for you, but you kept walking. Unless you've perfected the skill of being able to ignore me, it seemed like you never even saw or heard me." His eyes hold a genuinity inside, softening with concern as his bottom lip curls inward. Yet, I find it hard to believe he can care for me after what he did to me.

To think I had someone stand by me when the whole world was trying to bring me down, yet he was the one with the knife the entire time.

"Maybe you have perfected the art of ignoring," he mutters, but there's nothing for me to say in response. Nothing I want to say to him. A metallic taste of blood rises in my mouth, staining my teeth as they bite into the soft flesh of my tongue. Taking a harsh step to turn away from him, I move to walk away from having this conversation, from him. "Hey, please just talk to me," his hand brushes against my skin to stop me as I take another step away. As I feel his fingers make contact with my arm, I flick his hand away, the stinging of my teeth as they bear inside my tongue increasing.

"Stop," irritation bites in my words as I attempt to take another step. "I have to go."

Despite any wish I have otherwise, any desire there may be for circumstances to stand differently, the best thing I could do for myself now is walk away. Back in another life, a life before these hallucinations and before the accident, Finn would have been my knight to save me from these delusions. From these wolves. From myself. In another life we would have laughed together at the idea of me running from imaginary monsters and tripping on that stupid branch. But that was then, in that other life. This is now. And now? Too much has happened to even think of forgiveness.

"Let me at least drive you home," he persists, copying each step I make away from him.

"I'm not going home," the words muffle out instinctively. As my eyes keep on the faint light of the park, fear arises through me like a hurricane. A fear that there is no clear answer. That everything that is happening is more than I could possibly figure out by myself, and without answers, I will lose any sanity left inside. A fear that drives inside my gut, moving until there's a tight clenching in my chest as I realize what I need to do.

I need to see her.

I have to go to my mother.

Chapter 3

"Where are you going? I can take you," Finn says, still following inches behind me, his diligence clashing with my annoyance.

Too far. Damn it. Halting in my tracks, the continuous swelling in my mind that shouts at me to keep walking stills as the realization sets in that I have no choice. Any other option will be too late in getting there, and what I have to do can't wait any longer. I have to do this, regardless of how. One car ride for me to get the answers I need, I have to.

A sigh escapes with a heavy breath, a simple indication followed by a quick nod in agreement. Without missing a beat, Finn closes the short gap between us to now walk besides me, guiding the two of us to his car.

As we reach his car after an eternal voyage, the torment of my mother and the memory of our accident stabs at every corner of my mind abates, being replaced with a separate affliction of having to be in the same space as Finn. Opening the door to the passenger side, Finn starts the engine of his car and pulls up the navigation app on his phone.

"Where am I taking you?"

"The institution," the words play gently from my lips and Finn remains silent, typing the address into his keyboard.

The thought of seeing her again dreads inside me, especially since the last time was a month after she was taken away—my first birthday without her. It was the most horrifying thing I've ever had to do, seeing her where she was and knowing why she was there. Everything happened right before my fifteenth birthday; a time where I should be enjoying high school events, hanging out with friends, readying myself for the next journeys I'll take in this world. Instead, I became afraid and shut myself out from the world. It's been nearly three years, but what happened to me will haunt me forever.

My last visit rings vividly in my mind. "Everything is going to be alright," she told me, and I actually believed her. That was until her next words were a warning to "never let the howls turn to words." That's what led to that being my last visit, only dropping by to leave gifts for holidays or birthdays. But I haven't seen her since.

I used to write letters, sometimes even poems I jotted down during classes, but over the years I stopped writing. It was easy to believe all her babble was nonsense, but now with everything that's happening, I don't know. It's funny, looking at myself now. After all these years, I'm in the same straightjacket as her. The question is; am I going crazy, or is she actually sane? Can this still be nonsense? Whatever the case, I'm finally ready to listen, desperately hoping for answers.

After a few moments in the car, Finn lowers the music that had been playing from the radio. "I'm sorry. You know I never intended to hurt you." A soft sadness tints his words. "I miss you."

Finn has always missed me. Whether I was hiding out for a few days after a fight with my parents, or even missing a day of classes. Before everything, I would have said with full certainty that Finn was the greatest person I know. Until he turned out to be like the rest. What he did cut deeper than any of the words people spewed out at me. How they claimed if my mother's insane, I must be too, joking about her breakdown as if it were some comedic sitcom.

When I say the incident ruined my life, I really fucking mean it.

"I'm not doing this with you," I say, my voice drained of any emotion at this point. It's not the time to be playing this game with Finn, not when I know what I have to do in a few moments.

"What am I supposed to do, Serelia? I keep trying to talk to you, but every time I do you walk away. I don't know how to fix this, how to make you forgive me."

"I don't want you to fix this, you can't. Not once did you stop the name-calling or torment. You laughed at their jokes despite calling me your best friend. You're the one who left me for her. That's not on me." I don't know if he started the rumor or not, or even if it was his girlfriend. Either way, he didn't have anything to say in my defense. Sometimes silence is as bad as starting the rumor.

As soon as I finish speaking, he pulls up into the parking lot and I practically jump out of the car before he fully stops. Looking up, all I can see is the institution.

A second car door shuts and there's a sound of footsteps against concrete.

Finn moves around the car, stopping in front of me, blocking my view of the hospital as it awaits ahead. "Is there anything else you need? Do you want me to go in with you?"

"There's nothing for you to do in there," my eyes peer past his head, trained onto the neon, scarlett words that hang above the door. I'm not sure if it's the uneasiness of having to go inside that sends a tight bile that scratches within my throat, or the dread of not knowing what answers she'll have for me when I do make it inside that welts across my abdomen, but any hint of resentment and anger I feel for Finn dissipates as my eyes flick back onto his in front. "Thanks... for the ride." The words struggle as they reach my lips from the shock waves that signal across my being, the aching as every bit of me wants to shut down here in the parking lot and never have to face what is to come.

A small smile settles upon his face. "That's the first nice thing you've said to me in months. Don't worry about it, I'm always here for you." As he says those words, I turn my head downwards avoiding his gaze, it takes every bit of strength I have not to talk to Finn. To pretend like everything is okay between us. "Can we just talk, for a moment?"

"Thanks for the ride, I'll find my own way home." I mutter, spinning on my heel to face him. Though it's clear Finn is trying, now isn't the time for continued mannerisms and long talks. "There's nothing else to say, Finn. I have something to do."

Beginning my journey away, Finn doesn't say anything else. The only challenge I face is the one lying in front of me.

Here goes nothing.

A sign that reads 'Home For Angels' hovers above. Taking a deep breath, knowing what awaits inside, I question whether or not to turn back. Doubt clouds my mind and I wonder if leaving now will allow me to live in blissful ignorance. One voice shouts inside me to turn around and hope this problem will disappear, another whispers to stop being stupid and go in.

Giving into the smaller voice, I walk to the prison-like hospital. I have no choice, that is, unless the wolves want to stop speaking in riddles and say something pertinent. Noticing the bars on the window, part of me believes that if I walk inside now, I'll never escape.

For whatever reason, she has the answers I need, which is the only way I gain enough courage to continue forward. Whatever is happening is not a coincidence. Maybe I am going insane, that this depression and anxiety is finally taking its hold over me completely, but I have to know for sure. Either the answer is that I am truly insane, or there is so much more going on behind the scenes in my life and I need to learn the script.

Heading to the front desk, a nurse sitting at the front desks looks up and asks me the general questions for visitors. Her kind smile registers within me, that is, until I mention her name. The nurse's face drops and pity shines in her eyes. Everyone here knows the story of her and I.

A warming smile turns to a questioning and professional tone as she hands me a visitor's pass with my name, ID picture, and the numbers forty-two next to the letter 'D' in a bold, white font. With concern as I ready myself to leave to her room, the nurse offers a guard to accompany me, to which I politely reject and follow with a 'thank you.' Though, it did bring some worry, the nurses thinking I would need someone to protect me, even though she's locked up here. How insane is she truly?

My finger twitches against the elevator button as it glows white. The doors open and my stomach sinks and the knot in my chest tightens as I walk inside, pushing the button for the fourth floor.

Turn back now. You don't have to be here. If you continue, things will only get worse. I keep walking, shoving any resistance my mind and body have deep down. The room numbers blur by until I find the one that holds her inside. Through a small window on the door I can see her. Last chance. Turn back now or go inside. This is it.

It's too late to turn back now. I have to go to her.

Turning the knob on the door, my feet slowly step inside. The beating of my heart has ceased, all my thoughts have faded from existence. It's her and I. Or, at least, a being that represents her. In her eyes is the same ghostly and hopeless stare I see whenever I look in the mirror. Though mine was caused by the accident, hers is from after. It's the result of ten pills a day and constant sedation flooded into her veins through I.Vs. It takes me a moment to realize that this is a person, and not just some statue that is designed to look like her. It's her.

She doesn't notice my presence until I stand directly in front of her, but as soon as she does, life comes into her drained eyes and her corpse skin gains color back into it. As if seeing me has brought her back from the dead.

My feet shuffle, unsure of how to position myself, as an awkward voice registers when I say, "Hi, Mom."

Now that I'm here, all I want to do is run away. Part of me wants to jump into her arms like a child and have her tell me everything's okay, the other never wants to see her again and leave this place as a distant memory.

Then, all I see is her.

My mother.

Stress has aged her despite her relative youth. Frown lines and crinkles indent in her face, with a sagged smile and shoulders that slump in her chair. Somehow, she still looks as beautiful as the woman I see in my polaroid and I know that my mother is still there.

"Serelia?" Her body perks up, yet her voice remains frail. "Where have you been? How are you? I've missed you!" Though life is brought into her eyes, her body is tired and idle. Time dawns on me of how long it has been, and more importantly, how much I have missed my mom.

Remember what you are here for. Remember what is important. A switch flips on in my brain and a memory revisits the truth—the reason why she is in here. How she almost killed me in a car accident because she claimed the wolves were speaking to her. That she became another person who abandoned me.

Still, I can't help but love her.

"I'm okay. I've missed you too. How are you?" My voice cracks with each word, my throat holding back a sob. I can't tell if it stems from anger or sadness at this point. I need to figure out how to get the answers I came here for. Her hand reaches for mine, a frail pressure that is lighter than a paper. Touch of death. A cold rush clashes with her warmth, a lost soul trapped inside a graying corpse. If I were to move my hand even an inch, it's possible her hand will crumble above.

"I'm doing better." Though her voice is weak, the same love and childish glee can be heard. "The doctors say I'm getting healthier. They gave me all of your letters, every single one. Seeing you now too, I realize how beautiful and smart you have grown to be. I'm so proud." A sad smile rises on my face as I look into her eyes, tears well, but I remain strong for her. "I've missed getting more of your letters. I can't remember how long it's been since the last." She pauses, something in her mind clicking. "Are you sure you're okay? Why have you come today?"

Now or never. Closing my eyes, I suck in a deep breath, before letting out, "Actually, there is something I need to ask you." Glancing down, she sits quietly, and the nerves tingle upon my skin. I don't know if I can face this, any of this.

"What is it? You're making me nervous."

Building up every ounce of strength I have, I force myself to look back up to her. I need to see her eyes when she hears what I have to ask. "I've been having nightmares, the only thing is, I don't think they're just that." I pause, a faded memory hazed in my mind. "You used to tell me stories. When I was little, you told me about a forest. I think that's what I've been seeing in my dreams, that place. The wolves..." My words soften as I continue, unable to form a question on my hesitant lips. Realization strikes like a blade, if I hear the wolves, if this forest was real, then I blamed my mother for nothing. How can I ask her for the truth for the exact thing I have blamed her for being insane about? My eyes wander back to her, refocusing my attention from my fears and onto her, only to find her now filled with fear. "Mom?"

Shaking like a leaf in the wind, her eyes that were previously vacant are now darting around the room as she mutters insensible words under her breath. Her fragile hand grows taut over mine, her emaciated fingers wrapping around mine, I can feel each edge of each bone digging into my skin.

"This wasn't supposed to happen. The deal, he's breaking the deal." Her sentences don't come out whole, the only coherent words being 'he' and 'deal.'

"What deal, Mom? Who are you talking about?"

Though, to no avail, her mind becomes trapped around the same shortened phrases, repeating ramblings over and over. Is this what's going to happen to me? My fingers reach for her arm, barely making contact with her quivering body before she draws her eyes to mine.

Her words repeat over and over again. My fingers place upon her arm and she turns her focus back to me, fear spreading across her face. "Serelia, you have to leave. Getaway, don't listen to him. You can't! You're not safe." In no warning, a shrill pries from her throat, filling the room is a terrifying scream. There's a break in her throat, the sound of her vocal cords ready to snap from her piercing cry. The sound wavers against my skin, leaving behind a trail of goosebumps, true fear filling this room in every possible way. "Leave her alone! Don't take her! Please!"

My eyes widen and I pull my hand away as she thrashes in her chair. She screams, a terrifying noise I've only heard once before. Panicking, I stand and back up, paralyzed by the person in front of me. Memories of the accident resurface, reliving each painful memory as if it was happening all over again. Like the storm is happening and I'm about to end up in the same position as before.

It's happening again.

As my feet shuffle back some more, my mind blank from panic, my mother leaps forward. "You have to run, Serelia! Escape, don't let them take you."

Her words barely register in my ears, a yelp escaping my throat as her hand clings around my wrist. The digging of nails sinks into my skin, a warm rush of blood flows down my wrists and onto the white tile below. She claws her fingers deeper into my arm, my eyes nearly shut from the pain but I force myself to look at her. To see her eyes. Only fear holds inside them, brown eyes spellbound by this alarm, her pupils drowning out life into a black nothingness.

"You're hurting me," my voice whines out, but her grip only tightens. Pulling my arm away becomes impossible, each attempt followed by a deeper stinging from her grip of death. Acting as if she's in a trance, she continues on her hysterical ramblings and her nails pressure so deep they may soon hit the bones of my wrist. "Mommy, please."

Tears fall from my eyes. A seventeen year old girl thrusted back in time to fourteen. Three years ago the same words spilled from my mouth, right before we ended up in a ditch on a forsaken highway. Like now, my words have no effect on her.

Insanity has once again taken my mother away from me.

Nurses start to pour in, a few behind me, trying to pull me away from my mother. Others attempt to calm her, but to no avail, she ends up with a needle in her arm, falling limp into the pool of white scrubs. Her hand descends down to her side, the strain on my wrist still there though. A phantom of her grip on me.

The nurses drag me out, their words muffled in my ears. Ignoring them, I run to the elevator as fast as my legs are able. Questions flood through me, speeding as quick as the adrenaline in my blood. The elevator barely has the chance to make it to a second floor before my patience is lost, rushing to the emergency stairs instead.

I need to get out.

Flying down the stairwell, I shove my way past the doors. Her words replay over in my head. "You're not safe," I mutter to myself. That's twice I've heard those words now. What am I not safe from?

My hand brushes against my wrist, the touch tender as my fingers cover in blood. Instead of answers, I'm leaving with more questions. A fear churns inside of me that my mother is simply insane, and that I'm becoming the same. Still, I believe there is more out there. That even after everything that just happened, this is all too much of a coincidence and something bigger is calling out to me. The whispers are calling to me.

What am I supposed to do now?

It's been a week since my visit with my mother. One week since she transformed from a statue-like being to someone who knew nothing but fear. Her horror seemed to push away my own, for I have not had a nightmare since the visit. One week of peace, of whispers faded and my head not weighed down by a forest or wolves. My leg has for the most part healed, still some bruising and slight pressure, but manageable. Sleep was still elusive to me, worry filling my being every time I closed my eyes and questions stirring in my brain.

Tonight, though, something changes as I drift to sleep.

I see him. He stands there at the edge of darkness. His features shine in the moonlike, brown eyes as chilling as before, lips a thin line, pale skin against the faint light. A smirk forms on the corner of his mouth, he's waiting. He knows something is changing. I stand in a deafening silence, shaky breath teasing through the forest, conjuring a foggy air that clashes back against my skin. Cold sweat runs down my back, my knees shake and my body sways.

Coughing in an attempt to steady my breath, a whisper muffles. "Who are you?" Nothing. "What do you want from me?"

"You know why you're here." His words break the silence, though his lips never move. "We don't have time for questions, return before it is too late. We are waiting." With this, I realize that though he is speaking, his words are sounding in my head. Like the wolves and their whispers, none of it feels real. It's all in my mind.

Before I have a chance to respond, he looks back into the darkness. Something moves behind him, a second figure. Someone else is here.

Emerging is another man, a bit shorter than the first. Yet his being screams power, someone much stronger. A new sense of recognition strikes me as he steps into the light. My eyes draw straight to him, an older man staring right at me. An unrecognizable sadness places within me. I know this man.

That's impossible.

A single word barely escapes my throat as I stare at the figure in front of me.

"Dad?"

Chapter 4

<hr>

A force draws my legs forward, the unbelief of my face in front of me. Green eyes piercing into my own, the ember green I've only ever seen in my reflection, studying me. They absorb the features of my face, all the while I do the same to him. There's no way. To see his face without so much of a picture, let alone my memories.

How is he here?

Why is he here?

My brain struggles to comprehend this, thinking perhaps it might be easier to believe this is a work of my imagination at play, concocting a father after the realization set how far gone my mother may be. How far gone I may be. But deep down, with the entirety of my being, I know that this is as real as it gets. That this man is him. That in front of me stands the person who had left me years ago, and a long-gone nostalgia crashes into me. A longing sense overwhelming as I stare at him, his face.

My father's face.

In all those weakened moments when I wanted a father to whisk me away from this insanity, to save me after the accident despite what he's done, I used to imagine him. I mean, it's not like you ever want to imagine the person who left you, but still, you can't help but wonder. And in all that wonder, this is the face I had seen.

The darkness around begins to fade, the trees shrinking to a vision gone smaller, swallowed by a menacing fog. A veil of my dream yanking away the scene around us. I'm not ready to go. I finally am seeing the man who shares my blood, my eyes. I'm not supposed to wake up, not yet. I need more time.

The questions that crumple inside my brain scream in the back of my throat, but my jaw hangs too heavy to form any sentence past my lips. I don't know whether to plead with him not to go, or remember this is only a dream that can be forgotten with a pinch. A wispy fog envelops and smoky tendrils wrap around, a thin haze spreading across our feet before rising tall until it's the two of us. Everything vanished into an indiscernible gray, a gray similar to the one hazing over my mind.

He smiles, one soft and reassuring, letting that be the last thing I possibly will ever see of my father before he is swallowed by a sea of mist.

My eyes snap open, sweat covers my pillows and dampens across my face, blending with the tears that are still leaking from my eyes. My breath catches in my throat, a tightening in my stomach wrenches inside as I sit up. Green eyes engraved into my vision, tearing through its surface like a stained memory. The single word once again falls past my lips: "Dad."

A pull within hauls me from my bed, pulling me to do something I've always been afraid to do before. Walking through the hallway, I stop in front of her door. Don't do it, you're letting your dreams win. They aren't real. Turn around, you don't have to do this. Remember the difference between reality and insanity. But what if reality is insanity?

The cold metal of the door knob bites into my fingertips, sending a shiver through me, a final warning that if I go forward, there is no turning back. Yet I turn the doorknob anyway, opening the door of my mother's room and likely sealing my fate, my ultimate shove into the madness.

Visions of our past dance along the room that hasn't aged, has never changed since the moment she was taken away. Following the boards that form their own brown wooden path, they take me to a frame that holds my mother's memories, a closet stuffed with my last true memories of her. Tossing out every piece of clothing, every kept trinket of a stored away memory, every scrapbook and picture, shuffling through each document and box stuffed inside, I scramble and search every object.

A distant voice of my mother ringing inside my head, telling me how despite his absence, her heart's beat for him never hesitated, never faded. How every single night since he desert-ed her, she felt his presence in this one photo she could never tear, burn, or throw away. A photo I've never had any interest in, before now at least. It was always so much easier to pretend he didn't exist, to try to pretend he didn't exist. That way, I was never weighed down by the anger or sadness of him. And now my mother is gone, or at least gone to the point where each time I want to see her involves a visitor's pass and having to watch drugs being pumped into her.

A part of me wishes I could forget her instead of forgive, to try and pretend our past is nothing more than history we all eventually forget, but I know that she never gave up on me, not intentionally at least.

Tearing through the boxes, scanning all the pictures trapped inside, I come across one scrapbook with the words 'Beats as One' sprawled across in black marker. Tugging it from the bottom of the cardboard box, photos spill out, pictures of me scattering across the floor in front of me. Time reverses the further I flip, from a young me to my pregnant mother. Images of her when she was around my age and some of when grandma was her age. Then I reach the end and I see it. I see him.

A small polaroid carries a snapshot of my mom standing beside a boy around her age. Immediately I recognize him from the man in my dreams, granted he's a bit younger here, but his eyes are exactly the same. His arm rests across her shoulders, her head lies on his, they look so relaxed next to each other, so normal. My eyes carry down onto her stomach, a small bump faintly seen from the figure of her dress, this must be right before he left. Flipping the polaroid around, white marker covers the back of the film: 'Aryce, Abria, and Baby Lone - 5 December 2001.' About five months before I was even born, and by my birthday, 26 April 2002, he was gone.

The whispers sound, drawing out any conflict pacing in my brain. Then their words transform, I hear them drawing closer and closer, so close that they could be right behind me. Their words grow louder until they are no longer words at all, but rather a mournful howl chorusing all around me I can't ignore.

Through the cries of the wolves, a voice rises above. So many questions, Serelia. When will you understand there are no simple answers? It's him, my father. I know it is, the same way I had known his face. His voice is firm and resonant, like a rising storm, one that makes the hairs creep along the back of your neck, all somber and serious. You know what you must do. The map to finding me is already within you, listen to your instincts. I'll be here waiting.

As his voice disappears and the echoes fade, the howling begins to die down, quieter and quieter until there's nothing, like a deaf man in a ghost town, or a person in a psychiatric cell, padded from every wall. A twisted pain strains inside my chest making it difficult to breathe, surges of anxiety and panic overwhelm. For a moment, I get lost in his eyes, trying to conjure up why he would ever need me, why now? Focus.

Standing up with the picture anchored between my fingers, leaving the remaining, forsaken remnants of my mother's room behind, I tread back through the halls. The floor feels heavier this time, or maybe it's my feet, trudging through wooden floors as if they were waves. Or maybe tar, trying to drown me under a cool and weightless world below.

"Hey sweetheart, are you okay?" Her eyes trail to the photo in my grasp.

"Everything's fine," I say, perhaps a little too quick in response. "I was trying to find something for a project I'm doing and found this picture I liked."

Truth is, I won't know how she'd react to me looking through mom's photos, especially one with my dad in it. Instead, it might be easiest to bend the truth.

Despite a questioning look in her eyes, furrowed eyebrows and a crinkle in her forehead, she doesn't push any further. "Okay," she pauses. "Do you want anything for lunch?"

"I'm okay. Thank you."

Still with her questioning gaze, her eyes visibly bouncing between my own, she turns to go back downstairs. I know that it must be hard for her. It is my mother entrapped in the institution, but sometimes I forget that it's also her daughter. More than that, instead of being able to move on or grieve or do whatever any sane person would do in such a situation, she has to take care of me. Grandma has her own stories, has fought her own battles. Watching as she descends down the stairs, I try to remind myself it's not only me who feels the burdens of insanity—whether it's living with it, or probably worse, seeing someone you love live with it.

Crutching onto the picture still tight in my grasp, I close the bedroom door behind me and head for my desk. Pushing open the laptop that sits on top of some old homework and papers, I prop up the photo against the lower corner of my screen.

"Lupa...Valley...High...School," the words mumble between my lips as I simultaneously type them onto the keyboard. Clicking on the Alumni page, a series of students whose surname begins in 'A' fill the screen in a lined order. Looking up the name 'Aryce' and the year I know my mom graduated there, my finger flutters as it pushes against the Enter key.

An image pops up on the laptop, my eyes immediately catching the scintillating green eyes that stare back in the pixels. 'Aryce Bade.' His picture so clear in front of me, the man who I saw less than twelve hours ago. It's him. He really exists, somewhere in the real world and not only in my dreams. He's real.

Studying his features, zooming in on his face and taking in every pixelated letter of the information under his profile. At least the information the Alumni page gives you, and I print out the page. Then curiosity takes over before my brain can catch up with my fingers as they type out 'Abria Lone' in the search box next.

Aside from her darker eyes, I finally get a bit of understanding on what people mean when they say we look as if we were twins. Probably not to that extent, but I leer at her picture. How she looks so different than she does now, not only younger, but happier. A genuine smile behind eyes, a life years ago when she had no clue what would soon become her future. I miss you so much. I wish I could've known you like this. How did everything change in you so quickly?

If only all of this insanity within me can finally bring you back to me.

Readjusting my focus back onto the screen, a new thought pops into my head back to my visions- the twisted branches of the thick greenery surrounding, the gardens of flowers all of varying colors, dulled by the night sky painted with glistening drops of heaven and a hanging crescent above.

Though I can't say for sure if it's real, the forest, or where it would even be, I know what it looks like from my dreams. Maybe. Just maybe. Clearing the current search tab, I type in 'Forests in Lupa Valley.' Zero results found. Widening the search, I type in, 'Forests in Oregon,' and unsurprisingly the amount of results spans pages and pages of sites. This is going to be difficult.

Opening up the first few images to find anything that may bring any sort of recollection, I press the arrow key and inspect each image closely. After a few or more images, a ringing sounds, building up the more images I go through. It reaches the point where the sound resonates into my brain, a blur crosses through my sight and forces my eyes shut. Scratching my nails against the wooden desk before gripping the end to anchor myself, a pulsation moves through my veins.

An image appears before me, though my eyes remain closed. The pulsations become pain, a bullet shooting past each organ in my body, as if it were tearing each and every blood cell, freezing their movements before melting and soon burning beneath my skin. At first, there's nothing but meshing colors fighting a battle in my brain. Clearing up, a vivid picture focuses to reveal the place that haunts and intrigues me all at once—the forest.

The smell of trees fills my noses with each breath. The sound of a river, trickling through the stream across the dirt, unknowing how far it reaches. A gust of wind brushing my skin, causing my hairs to rise and shiver as it touches the grass below. A canvas in my mind more real than any image online.

Then, as quick as a snap, my eyes open and I'm back in my room as if nothing ever happened.

Chapter 5

Though now the whispers call out louder, a siren's song luring me to stand. Tempting the muscles in my calves, blood pooling through them, to run. Outside the door with no hesitation, not a single thought was able to rise above the whispers. They sing, bewitching my body, yet not one coherent word to be made out. Even as grandma's muffled voice can be heard from behind, my speed quickens as I hustle through the neighborhood and into the city ahead.

The whispers acting as a ventriloquist with invisible strings, I have no control of my body. The forest flickers across my sight, and before there's any realization of what's happening, the unseen strings attached to me are torn and my body crashes to the ground. A person hovers over me, my vision adjusts, shifting their being into a familiar someone.

"Guess I should say it's nice crashing into you," Finn's deep voice rings above as my body remains on the cold concrete.

"It's becoming a habit for me to find you on the ground like this," his hand reaches down, offering itself to help me up.

"Sure it is," mock laces my words, and as I lock my sight onto his open hand, temptation nearly gives in to accept it. But if I did so, I'd not only be accepting his hand, but his friendship once again. Ignoring his gesture, I twist my body to the side and push myself up. Though, as stubborn as I may be, so is Finn, despite my moving away from his grasp, he bends down anyway. Grabbing my upper arm when I push myself up, he helps to pull me up until I'm able to regain my balance.

"How did everything go?" He begins to ask, the words, 'with your mom,' itching at the tip of his tongue. Though, there's a stuttering break before he finishes his sentence, the clear hesitation and recognition of that not being the conversation starter he thinks it is. "Did you hear what's happening with school?" He seems to take my silence as a gesture for him to continue. "Some pipe burst or whatever and now the classrooms are flooded, a majority of them at least." Boredom twines in his voice as he recalls the information, but he still goes on. An excuse to talk to me without me leaving. "Not really sure how true that is, just rumors from others at least. The school did send an email, though, saying for whatever reason, they can't open physically until the situation is handled and ensure safety for students. However all that goes."

"What about classes?"

His shoulders tug upwards, "Who knows, switch to online, maybe? Extremely extended weekend?"

Well, it's one less thing to worry about. Between packing up the rest of my stuff to move soon and whatever this is, this whole forest-whisper-insanity thing, not needing to stress over AP English and senior Calculus will be a nice change. Colleges are something I took care of early on, applying as soon as applications opened. Not a single one near a hundred miles to Lupa Valley, or even in the state of Oregon. It truly is the only hope of any decent future I could have, leaving.

"Hey, Ser," Finn mutters, causing me to avert my eyes back to him. "Look." His hand reaches into the pocket of his hoodie, bringing back out a paper box of chocolate-covered peanuts. My favorites—our favorites.

"Really?" I eye the candy, my eyebrow raised, before looking back to him. He unfolds the top, flicking one into his mouth while keeping my gaze, a smile sorted on his lips as he chews.

"C'mon," he pushes the chocolate to me. "If you don't eat one, my feelings are gonna be hurt."

"They're melted," I tease when peeking inside, yet still grabbing the box from his hand and pouring some onto my own.

"Still tastes the same," gleam beams in his eyes watching me bring one to my mouth.

And for once, I allow myself this moment. A moment of actual niceness with Finn. Like old times. Able to ignore the whispers, the wolves, the visions to each candy with a boy I've known from before the wolves dictated my life.

The decency of this moment is quickly interrupted with a muffled beeping in the same pocket he pulled the candy from.

Catching Finn's body stiffening for a second, his hand reaches back into the pocket to reveal his phone with a screen cracked beyond any other person being able to see it with ease. Something I've always joked with him for, his lack of maintaining a device with no scratches or cracks for at least a month. Still, like now, he refuses to use a case.

His fingers begin to jump across the screen, and whether it be because of the close gap between us or from pure curiosity, I glance down, able to make out him typing 'nothing important' before pushing send. Unaware of me looking at his screen, Finn continues to text and my eyes dart to the top to make out the name of the person on the other end—Maeve.

I knew our brief moment was over and I remember why I had cut Finn from my life in the first place. My place in his life—nothing important. Even now, as I back away with a silent scowl across my face, my body hardening as much as my emotions, he fails to notice. Though I lack knowing what the full context of his message may have been, the words still ring true to everything between us and it becomes a switch to bring me back to the real world.

Turning to take a step away is when his eyes must realize the shift of my mood. "What's wrong?" His voice questions from now behind me, his hand placing on mine to turn me back towards him.

"Nothing, I'm fine." A cold bites onto my hand as I tug it from his, despite the warmth outside. The whispers take residence in my mind once again as I once again ready myself to turn away from him.

"Serelia, please. What happened?"

"Nothing important to you," my words mimic his text. "Finn, I don't have the time nor do I even want to stand here with you and act like all is fine with us. I don't want to hear what you have to say. No explanations, or apologizes, nothing. There's nothing you can do to fix us back to what we once were." His flinches at my words don't go unnoticed by me, but I go on. The whispers grow, causing my words to fly from my mouth with no thought to them. "Do whatever the hell you want, but don't involve me. Please."

My gaze lingers, waiting for him to say something, anything to make me want to forgive him and stay. He doesn't. And once more, I turn my back on yet another reminder of my past.

Racing back to my house, head down watching each step and my mind on overdrive, I try to calm myself. For hours, hell weeks, I am losing my grip on sanity. A man who I absolutely have no memories of shows up, not in person, but in my fucking dreams. The whispers of the wolves constantly buzzing in my mind, never quieting even for a minute. The more I try and try to ignore it, the stronger it comes back to bite me in the ass.

Reaching my front yard, not even having been an hour since I ran out of here, I find the door still wide open, grandma moving throughout the kitchen and living putting things in boxes and cleaning up the near-empty rooms. I had barely managed to avoid her questions not too long ago, but now after running out as if a maniac was chasing me, or rather I was a maniac, there will be no avoiding her. I don't know how much longer or how many more questions I can take before my silence crumbles beneath the weight of my secrets.

Rather than going through the front door, I sneak around the house and to the backyard. Placing my grip on the tree that towers outside of my room, I climb, but pass the unlocked window and go all the way until I can step off onto the roof.

My hiding spot. One where I've come to escape everything and everyone for as long as I could ascend the tree without falling or getting caught. And though it's not a million miles away and isn't exactly a masterful hiding spot, I've always loved the views.

The hues of orange, yellow, and red all rise to cast away darkness each morning. Cool breeze fighting against the sun's warmth. Birds chirping, a calming alarm, and a smell of wet dew covering the fresh-cut grass. Light conquers the sky with nothing able to take it away for these beginning hours. Not even the darkest of nightmares.

Then every night, a new world materializes. The sun allows itself to fade behind the endless skies and darkness surfaces until it devours every last bit of orange and gold. Purples, pinks, and blues now replace the once light colors, but not once do they feel daunting as they soar. They're mysterious, enchanting, waiting for the moon to take its throne.

Then in the quiet hours of our small part of the world, light and dark collide. Navy fills the sky while drops of the sun's tears are left behind. Golden-white lights scattered across, dancing around the moon above that casts a shadow over everything that once was.

Silence. Complete and utter silence. Your senses take in all of the nature around, adrenaline rushes through your body with the breeze as darkness takes over.

To me, these have always been my favorite times, my favorite views. Instead of the fight between light or dark you can share them both. Like the good and evil that inevitably rests in every soul. While some may prefer the light and fear the dark, and others will seek mystery over familiarity, it is the reality that this is the true game of life and all that makes up humankind.

One fails to exist without the other.

Without day, there is no adventure or learning or experiences to be achieved. There are no here and now moments. Without night, there is no rest, no dreams, no resets and fresh starts. There is no such thing as tomorrow.

In harmony, the two forever create life. Day and night are a path between life and death—beginning and end. With the yesterday, today, and tomorrow that each produces, a new story can be told.

And now, as I once again sit up onto this spot, midday soon to turn to night and the blues begin their overtake on the yellows, a city of a hundred lives passes below me. The houses emanating faint lights from their porches, the street lights adding their own glow. A darkened figure creeps from the shadows, its silhouette starting to take form under the light, yet before ever reaching, stops. A longing sensation calling me to it.

The sound of a broken branch cracks off to the side from the tree that perches next to my house. Yet nothing appears near. Drawing my eyes back to the shadow, realizing it's disappeared sends chills through me.

Choosing to ignore it as the insanity brewing within me, I spend a few more minutes looking out to the horizon. A sky full of stars being mimicked by porch lights from darkened houses. The thoughts looming of the haunted forest, and a face that seems to scare me more.

Chapter 6

The annoying repetition of my alarm clock and its maddening beeping grows louder, informing me that it's six in the morning. Though, without having slept a wink all night in fear of the nightmare's return, I had already known the time.

Besides, it hadn't been a peaceful night with the hollowing whispers outside of my window. A collection of "he's here for her," and "can he convince her?" Along with, "she needs to be ready. Red is coming." And the most eerie that has yet to leave my mind, "Serelia's blood will soon be spilt."

Scenarios play off in my mind, trying to figure out the situation. Either it's the obvious idea that I'm insane and it may have stemmed genetically from my mother. Another part of me may believe it's some curse placed upon me. Or the largest possibility, anxiety is a bitch and life is one elusive joke.

The idea of having to go back to see my mother for answers strains inside of me, my hands forcing my pillow over my face in an attempt to suffocate myself from the world.

After going through my quick daily routine, finishing with placing the small ring my mother gave to me years ago onto my finger. A silver band encrusted with modest diamonds, the thin teardrop emerald in its center that glistens in the sun, like a fallen leaf. Three thin lines of silver wrap around across the gem, caging it to the band.

Even after the accident, I never have been able to take it off. I tried once, the day that the mental institution took mom away from our house. I had taken the ring and thrown it out by where we crashed.

An hour later I went back for it, my heart felt empty without it on. A naked feeling had rushed through me, a part of me was missing.

That was the last time I ever took it off.

Writing up a quick note to my technology-impaired grandma, I move to open the front door, startled by the person on the other sign.

"The hell," a smile twists onto my face as Levana holds her hand upwards where she was about to knock.

"Hey, I was about to- well you know," she chuckles under her breath, lowering her hand down to her side. "Anyways, are you ready to go?"

"For?" My thoughts question aloud before remembering. "Crap, the mall," my voice trails off seeing a frown tug down on Levana's lips.

"Yeah, and unless someone is dying or the world is going to be ending in the next three hours that no one's told me about," her brisk frown now turns to a sly smile, "then you're not getting out of it." Her eyes give an unspoken 'I dare you,' and I can't exactly tell her what my other plans would have been.

Your nightmares won't vanish after a trip to the mall.

And as cruel as it may be, mom will still be where she is tomorrow. Perhaps one normal day doesn't seem so bad, that is, if I can even remember normal.

"Okay," I nod, "let's go."

"Serelia," she grins, placing a sympathetic hand upon my shoulder. "It's cute you think that you have a choice."

"Free world," I wink while tightening my lips together, them tugging upwards in a quick smile.

"Not with me."

Finding ourselves at Mama Meg's, the bijou diner of this town, one of Lupa's only redeeming qualities, we wait in one of the booths for Meg. She's perhaps one of the few people I can truly stand in this town and is someone I admire more than anyone. Someone who I could talk to after our accident and never has treated me like a porcelain doll ready to shatter. Meg's been here for as long as anyone can remember, this diner standing just as long.

Such a compact establishment, assorted in a blend of greens, golds, browns, and reds, giving it a woodland-feel. Lanterns are the only source of light if not for the large windows in front. Elkwood chairs to match the tables, walls chipping old paint, and the grease that strains your nose as soon as you walk in. Though, that's never stopped Meg and her undeniable recipes.

Sitting a couple of waters in front of us, Meg sits beside me with a soft smile. Levana grows quieter, her leg bouncing beneath the table, bumping into mine every so often.

Furrowing my eyebrows at her sudden apprehension, Meg's frail voice breaks the quiet. "Hi girls, how are you both?"

Levana, remaining quiet, leaves me to speak up. "We're doing good, Mama," the word slipping out easier for Meg than it ever has for Abria. She's really been the most motherly figure I've had since the accident. "How are you?'

"Oh you know, the same old. Cooking faster than I can breathe, my lungs must be filled with grease fumes by now!" Turning my gaze from Levana to Mama, a smile forms onto my lips with a light chuckle that harmonizes with that of Meg's. "Levana, dear!" She beams across the table, "So quiet today! How are you, love?"

"I'm okay," she mutters, rushing her words in a quick breath, never turning to face Meg.

Moving in her seat, stiff as she shuffles and her hand reaches for her mouth, I bite my bottom lip to avoid calling out her sudden shift in mood.

Unsure if Meg picks up Levana's same uneasiness, she keeps her sight on Levana before turning back to me and switching between the two of us. "I'm sure you two must be hungry! I can cook you lovelies your usuals."

"Thank you, Mama," I say, nodding my head in her direction, still gracing a small smile before she turns to leave.

As soon as Meg is out of view, I shift my attention back to Levana, still tense in her seat. "What's going on? Are you alright?"

"Oh, yeah. Sorry, babes," she jumps up a bit, her hand quickly lowering back onto the table, almost as if she had forgotten I was here entirely. "I could've sworn someone was following us. I didn't see who exactly, but it's like I could feel them watching us. Whoever it was, they gave me the absolute creeps. I think he's gone though now."

Her eyes look past me towards the front door and window, scanning the outside as if checking to make sure the coast was clear of any lurking strangers.

"He?" I pause, the wolves whispers in my mind, their warnings in the night. He's here for her. Could it be the same person? "Are you sure? We can leave and go back home or something." I try to keep a calm composure in my voice, not wanting her to worry or think it is more than some creeper. I don't even know if it even is the same person. That would mean to suggest the whispers are true and someone is coming for me.

Shaking out of her trance-like state, Levana's light-hearted spirit seems to return to her smile as she once more fixes her posture and brings her eyes back to me. "I'm fine. I'm probably just spiraling, it's been a day."

"We all have them, it seems," I tilt my head while my shoulder draws upward. "I think a bit of crazy is essential to life at this point," I joke, though the words feel a bit too real as they release from my mouth.

The two of us eat the buffet of food Meg brings for us not long after our conversation. Every now and again, my mind drifts back to my mom, how much I need to go back to speak to her. The fact that she knows something I can't even seem to understand, but have no choice to find out.

After paying for our meals, Levana drives us to the mall. Every so often she grows quiet again, but plays it off as "a moment." Though it's clear something is off with her.

Having another one of these "moments," her attention shift changes outside of her window, causing the car to swerve. Panic doesn't hesitate within me, my reflexes reaching for the overhead hanger and a yelp releasing past my lips and into the world.

A tear of reality brings my vision back to the night of my mom and I, how fast it was before our worlds changed.

My head lunged forward, clashing with the dashboard in front, not even able to let out a scream. The highway that was lined with infinite trees became a haze. The car hurled my mother and I.

Once.

Twice.

Before I lost count.

Only stopping when we made impact with a tree downhill. Glass sank into my skin. Leaves and dirt made their way past what had used to be a door, but was now littered somewhere up on the hill. My world literally turned upside down. Blood rushed to my brain and leaked out of the gash along my forehead.

Blood dripped down my face from my arms and stomach. The taste of its metallic nature tracing along my lips, blending with the tears that dropped to the roof of the car.

Through time, those wounds had turned to scabs which then turned to scars. A forever souvenir of this moment.

Being woken up with lights shining above, brighter than any star yet much more distant, streaking passed me though I remained immobile.

My mother's screams, a ghost's wails sounding from a person still alive. Nurses calling out a hundred codes a minute, having restrained her to a gurney near mine.

"The wolves. It was the wolves." Her cries echoed against the hospital walls. Loud enough to drown out the sound of my own heartbeat. Even the feeling of it. My body numbed by pain. Not even able to sense the needles prodded into my veins, pumping a supply of drugs into me that could send anyone down the rabbit hole to Wonderland.

It took a week before I was able to realize I wasn't dead.

Though my heart was still beating, it bled like the rest of me.

And those would become scars that, though unseen, would never heal.

A passing car honks at us, nearly skimming their own vehicle, snapping Levana back into focus and straightening out the wheel, barely missing the driver as they flip us off.

"I'm so sorry," she takes a breath in, pulling the car off to the side of the road. "Someone was there. I saw someone in front-" her voice breaks as she tries to speak. "I thought- There was- I'm so sorry. I could've sworn," she glances back to the road where we nearly crashed to try and confirm what she saw was real.

Drowning in my own memories. Suffocating myself in fear. Blood drips onto my leg from the nails that sink themselves into my palms. A heart buried deep into my stomach, trying to claw itself back up with each beat. Trapped by a knot wound within my gut. The gasp of air my lungs struggle for, itching against my throat, yet is caught by the threat of a scream that refuses to let out.

My eyes burn with visions, tears threatening but never falling.

It isn't until I catch a glimpse of him in the side mirror of the car for my panic to pause to register his presence.

I would recognize his eyes anywhere.

Then everything releases.

Get out.

My breath releases in heavy pants, quickening after each. My body loses control itself, pawing to break out of the unmoving car. The distant noise of Levena calling my name, concern rising with her voice. The restraint of her arms forcing me back inside as I claw against the doorframe, trying to yank myself free. My voice begs to let go, pleading to be left alone.

Managing to loosen her grasp against me, I take it as my opportunity to thrust myself forward, plunging myself into the concrete road. Bringing myself onto my feet just as fast, my body hurls itself onwards before making contact with a guard rail, the metal biting into my bloody palms.

Below me, a forest expanding across. The same painful tingling returns. Familiarity replacing the horror that resides in my body only moments ago. The whispers now deafening in my mind.

A hand presses against my shoulder, forcing my gaze to break away from the endless trees to spot Levana edging towards me. Her eyes filled with concern, moving towards me as if I was a wild animal, prepared to run at the first threat of human contact. Though her eyes never tore from mine, she was still a distance away.

But whose hand did I feel?

Do not fear the darkness. The wolves urge me from below. My head turning back to the forest, a compulsion in my body to come forward. You will learn the truth soon enough.

"Serelia," Levana advances closer. "Are you okay?"

Without a second to think, my head shakes before speaking. "No."

That is all I need to break out of any trace freezing itself onto my body for me to run. Avoiding Levana's hand that tries to stop me from dashing past her, I run.

Snaking through the town, my lungs burning for a breath of the fresh that beats against my face and dances through my hair. But every attempt of breath is stopped by a harsh stone that presses against my neck.

Coming upon my house, my legs don't waver as they rush through and sprint upstairs. Even with the warmth that spreads across the house, mixed with the heated adrenaline that pours through me, a coldness latches itself to my skin.

My feet stumble upon themselves, a threat with each step to collapse. Shoving the door open that barricades my bedroom, almost breaking the wood off of its hinges, my body finally gives into the weight of fear and drops. My knees thud onto the planks below. The only sound from the sharp intakes of breath that strain against my heart. Tears that were scorching my eyes now make their descent across my face. My hands strangling my neck, before pushing through my hair and clenching into fists.

"What is wrong with me?" The sentence struggles against a single breath.

My sight catches onto a mirror resting upon the floor besides me, my eyes locking onto the mourning green reflecting back. His green.

Your mother almost killed you. Your father abandoned you. Your nightmares plague you. The whispers never leave you. Why do you even try to fight it? Telling yourself you're not mad. That you can find a happy future for yourself. That you won't become another statistic of the world that no one will try to remember. What is your point in trying?

A scream pierces the air. A scream so loud it causes a raging ring in my eardrums. A scream so powerful it bleeds through my throat as it escapes into the world.

Every ounce of pain releasing into the single sound. All my anxiety, my fears, my memories making their escape. Any chaos of my life matching itself into my oppressing scream.

My nails trace into my thighs, blood tracking across tan. My body lurches forward, my stomach curdling the nausea that boils inside from the pressure of the scream. My eyelids stitching themselves shut and a wetness staining across my mouth and chin as saliva and tears pool out. My brain bashing against my skull as my head violently shakes, my hair stringing across my face.

"I can't do this, anymore." I haul my body upwards, my head now facing the ceiling, pleading with whatever heavens and hells exist to please end this suffering.

Lowering my sight, it catches onto the fallen mirror beside me. My hands pounce towards it, seizing the cold glass before thrusting it against the wall ahead. Another fleeting wail fleeing from my lips as the glass shatters on impact.

Then, with one glance, one look into a piece of fragmented reflection, reality slips away from my fingertips before I ever had a chance to catch it.

Everything I've ever known, ever believed, disappearing into the dark depths of insanity. My mind submerging into the glass, tearing itself at the reflection looking back, there is no use trying to recognize what is real anymore.

A stillness washes over me, my breathing slowing as I focus on the image looking back.

My face has already been unrecognizable to itself. Yet despite the sullen bags that tug against my cheeks and the knotted hair on top of my head, the peculiar green of my eyes has always been constant.

Now they're changed. And though I can clearly see myself in the mirror, it is not my eyes looking back. My eyes.

They're golden.

Chapter 7

A knock breaks through the silence inside my room. My body jumping from its limp position on the ground, my eyes pulling away from the mirror.

Taking a second to compose myself, a voice muffles through the wooden door. "It's grandma," Rose says. "May I come in?" There's no doubt she had heard my scream or the smashing of glass against a wall, probably waiting to let me have my moment before coming up to check on me.

"One second, please." My eyes tear from the closed door, hoping that if I look back into the glass, it will be green that fills my eyes and not gold. Though, that hope is startled as the aurous yellow flickers back at me. "I tripped on my desk. I'm cleaning it up right now." The excuse plays out of my mouth, my fingers twitching through my hair trying to figure out what to do.

My green eyes now reminding me of a golden fire. Their intense gleam bouncing off the glass, flashing two lights where my eyes should be. The whites of my eyes dissipated and my pupils constricting at its sight.

I have the eyes of an animal. Of a wolf.

"Serelia, are you sure you're okay? Please, can you open the door?" Her voice is uneasy, my mind imagining her standing alone against the doorway, peering her ear against the harsh frame to hear any response. Guilt unfurls within me, fighting the impulse to let her in and tell her everything.

But as I stare at my own image, the word 'monster' echoes in my head. What would grandma think? Would she even see what I am if I opened that door? I can't risk finding out.

Go to Abria. Now.

Realizing my keys are likely somewhere downstairs and I won't have any time to search without grandma asking her questions, instinct drives me to dialing Finn's number. My finger hovers over the phone button, but desperation wins and presses down.

"I need a ride," my words shoot down the phone as soon as he answers. "Please, can you pick me up from my house?"

"Um- sure," his voice questions, but as soon as he replies, I hang up and yank myself up.

Opening the door, I'm immediately face-to-face with grandma. My eyes squinting down in an effort for her not to see them.

"Serelia," she breathes. "What's going on? Please, will you talk to me?"

Letting out a heavy sigh, my words sound just above a whisper. "I'm sorry, I can't right now. Finn... he wanted to hang out. I, um- I have to go right now. I'll be home soon." I pause. "I'll be okay."

The worry in her eyes burns onto my skin, not being able to imagine how she must feel. But I can not let her see me like this. Without saying anything else, my legs move to pass out of the bedroom and begin downstairs. Grabbing and placing on a pair of sunglasses as I slip by the entry table, I go out the front door and try to put as much distance between grandma and me as possible.

Finn's car pulls up as I reach the curb, never stopping as I open the car door and slide inside. Even with the shaded glasses, I focus my eyes as far away from Finn and keep them facing the tinted window.

"Serelia-" Finn begins, but stops before asking any question. He knows there's a high chance I won't give any full answer, that is if I even respond. "Where are we going?" He says instead.

"I need to go back to see my mom." His silence speaks louder than any words as he hesitates. "Please Finn," my head slightly twists towards him, but still enough to where he can't see my eyes. "I wouldn't ask if it wasn't important."

Though I had no reason to trust him, part of me will always look at him for protection.

Through the eerie silence of the car ride, the only sounds coming from the lowered radio and other passing cars through a closed window, my mind tries to work out what to say when I see her.

You're not safe.

The last words I heard from her the last time I came to visit. Right before she was dragged and drugged in front of me, all hints of my mothers lost in madness.

The hospital seems to tower higher each time I visit, a numbing welcome as I approach. As the car comes to a halt, my hand floats over the handle to open the door, trying to use any ounce of courage within me to go in there.

Noticing Finn's hand start to push the door, I chime out, "Wait here. Please. I'll be out soon if you stay."

I don't turn to look at him, but the sound of his door closing and him shuffling back into his seat tells me he'll let me do this for myself, though in a nonverbal agreement.

Releasing a burdening sigh, my tongue squishes between my teeth as I manage to step out of the car. My stomach buzzing with the swarm of a thousand wasps, warning me that I haven't reached hell yet and still have time to turn back.

After checking-in, my eyes still covered with the dark glasses, I follow the nurse into the back gardens where Abria sat, drinking from a mug and staring into a shallow pond. Peace in the unpeaceful.

My steps lag the closer I move to her and I pull down the glasses sitting on my nose, keeping them firm in my grip as I watch as the woman in front of me, with glassed eyes and a warped smile, doesn't even take notice of me.

"Hi," I bend to sit beside her, the word 'mom' choking in my throat. My heart aching as she turns to me, the only emotion surfacing in her eyes as they widen at the sight of me.

"Serelia... your eyes. It's happening. I didn't think it would happen so quickly. I told them to stay away." Her sentences jumble as she begins to speak in riddles. "Where there are a wolf's ears, wolf's teeth are near. When golden sight reigns, darkness will come to play."

Her hands scuffle across the bench top, the stone scratching the bottom of her hand and drips of blood beginning to paint across it. Her head jolting from side to side as the riddle repeats across her lips.

"Mom?" My hand brushes against hers, my fingers connecting with the tops of hers when her head snaps back up to me.

"I told them to stay away." Her face bears the emotion of a statue, but her words shake as she speaks, fear lacing her broken voice.

"Told who, Mom?"

"Him... the one who watches. Caesar. He never should have come near you." Her hand whirls around before clinging to mine, her grip tightening and meshing my knuckles together, blood struggling to reach my fingertips. Only securing stronger the more I try to pull away. "That's why this is happening. The spell... it was supposed to lock the wolf away. Not till you were eighteen, he said. He said the wolf needs to be locked away. He told me to make sure you don't end up here. That you can't unleash the wolf. He told me-" her ramblings grow the more she talks, her aberrant words filling my mind. Is this true? The question stirs inside of me before my conscience pushes it out with a struggling force. Of course not.

"You're like him, Serelia." Her words break me out of my lingering debate on how much of this I can believe. Abria's tales of wolves and magic. "Your father. I didn't believe it either, but he showed me! He changed the world for me. I wouldn't lie to you, Serelia. I wouldn't. I love you," her last words whisper out.

Tears pool in my eyes, but I blink them back, standing abrupt and nearly knocking Abria off the bench. I can't. No. I can't. My hand rips from hers, yanking so rough I almost thought I would see it being dismembered from my wrist. She reaches out towards me again, but this time I push her away.

"How can you see my eyes?" My words become reserved for I know no matter what the truth is, her truth is not going to help. But, she can see my eyes. Why?

"It won't happen all at once... the transformation." Her head tilts up to the evening sky, the moon beginning its cast down on our world. A full moon. "It will happen. Soon."

My chest tightens, all of the pain I've been bottling up since the accident breaking free, crashing over us like the same shards of broken glass that made their marks on my skin that night.

"You almost killed us," I spit out. "You saw a fucking shadow and you almost killed us. Now you're telling me...what? That I'm a goddamn werewolf? Like this is some fucking fairy tale? I thought, for whatever reason, you cared for me. But no, you only care about these delusional fantasies that you seem so desperate to shove into me. I don't know if you're trying to finish the job when you caused the accident, trying to kill me, or drive me insane so you won't be alone here anymore. I can't figure out why. You lost me. You lost your family, grandma still isn't okay if you've ever wondered that. You lost any touch of reality I thought you still had. You lost yourself. And now, it looks like I'll be sitting here beside you soon enough, and still all you do is go on about all of this nonsense. I can't, I don't want to turn into you, but what choice do I have? And to say that you love me? That hurts the most. You don't do all of this to someone you're supposed to love. You're supposed to be there for me. I'm supposed to have you with me, all this time. All these years. But you were here. You didn't try. Not for me. Never talked to me. Never wanted me. You weren't there!"

My chest rises in heavy pants, the tears I've been trying to hold back now spilling down my face. Her mouth gapes open, wanting to say something but words never come. Her eyes brim with tears, I don't care. I can't look at her anymore. I can't do this again, not with her. "You will not see me again."

Fleeing back to the car, I slam the door shut before a breathless sob escapes me. Finn's hand reaches out to mine, but pulls back before making contact. I can hear him stutter, wanting to say something but not sure what, before starting the car and driving out of the lot.

"Do you want to tal-" Finn begins, but is interrupted by me shaking my head with a muddled 'no.'

He pauses, letting in a brief inhale as he clears his throat. I can hear his mind spinning to clear the awkward air between us.

"I think you can use a hamburger," he says, a gentle smile tugging on his lips. "And a milkshake." I try to let out a small laugh, but it's broken up by my breathlessness.

My eyes gaze out the window, numb and wordless, as I try to gain control on my breathing as we pull up to Mama's diner. Placing the sunglasses back onto my face as we walk out, the tears subside and my lungs start to calm.

"Is Meg here?" Finn asks a waitress as we walk inside, sliding into an empty booth seat before picking up the menu.

"I think she's still out," the young girl looks around before asking for our order. As she walks away, Meg walks through the door and makes immediate eye contact with me. An urgency surrounding her.

"Dear, can you come to the back with me," she says as she reaches our table, placing her hand on my shoulder, her words quiet but rushed.

My legs wobble as I push myself out of the seat, not knowing how to feel about what Meg could want from me. But the way her eyes scan my sunglasses, as if trying to see past them, I know she has some answers for me. Answers to what, though?

Before she can lead me back, Finn stands beside me and gently pulls my hand back towards him. "Before you can object, I'm not letting you go there alone," he leans into me, his whisper tingling against my ear. His tense posture lets me know he's feeling off about Meg's tone as well.

I don't even bother to argue with him, instead nodding to acknowledge his response and we follow Meg into one of the back rooms. Stepping inside, the only light coming from the miniscule window by her desk, the twilight flooding the room as the sun sets. Papers plaster all around, the furniture worn out with tears along the fabric. Meg gestures towards the threadbare sofa with a creaky table in front of it.

"I know," her stern words break the nervous silence between Finn and me. "About you, what you see... what you hear." She pauses and my breath hitches inside. There's no way. The whispers? She can't.

Before speaking anymore, she grabs a folder from on top of her desk, never breaking eye contact with me, and takes out an old newspaper. 'Teen girl survives tragic car accident. Mother taken into custody. "It was the wolves!" Mother claims.'

Why does she have this?

"There have always been rumors of strange sightings in our forests," Meg continues as I keep my eyes on the article. "Creatures that transform at night, under the light of the moon. Wolf-men, they called them, half-man and half-wolf. Your mother knew the truth." I bring my gaze back up to her, ignoring the rapid thud inside my chest. "Your mother... She holds a special place for them in her heart. She loves you so much that it ended up costing her the same thing she was trying to protect. In a frenzy to protect you," she tips her head towards the paper clenched in my hands, never finishing her sentence but knowing I understood what she wanted to say. "She feared for you because she knew your fate. Losing herself in the process. But your mother, she isn't unhinged. In fact, she knows more than many do in their lifetime. And she was willing to give up her own life to ensure you had one."

A force tugs inside my limbs, my knees buckling despite me sitting down. The words inside me striking my body like an explosive. "What are they?"

"These beasts," Meg continues to direct, her tone steady with each word. "They have roamed the woods of Lupa Valley for centuries, once a native part of life. Having been one with the earth until they became feared. Hunted by the true monsters. Humans."

Finn shuffles in his seat while I lean closer, taking in every word Meg says.

"You have this ancient blood inside of you, Serelia. Passed down to you from your father. He and Abria tried to protect you the best way they could." The spell... Abria's words blend with Meg's. "Spells don't last forever. It can't hold who you are forever."

"Wait," Finn interjects with skepticism twined in his voice. "So what? We're supposed to believe werewolves exist? And moreso, her mom and dad are some of them?"

Rolling my eyes at Finn's cluelessness, Meg chirps up to his question. "Humans have always been ignorant; and no, only Serelia's father is what you would call a 'werewolf.' Her mother is human." My spine freezes over at her use of the word, hearing it aloud for the first time in my life. And the fact that it's coming from Meg, of all people, how is this real?

"No," my voice demands, stopping all of this nonsense before it can go on. The nightmares, the whispers, everything. "No... just no."

"Serelia, there will come a day very soon where you must fulfill your destiny. You will need to stop denying who you are and become one with the moon. Then, and only then, you will learn the truth behind the beast."

With a snap, my walls rise back up, shielding me into remembering this is nothing more than myth. The world is playing a game that I don't know the rules to. Standing up, Finn besides me and clearly not believing any of this either, I motion to move out the door when Meg wraps her fingers around my arm.

"Believe me or not, it doesn't matter. You will see clearly soon." Rising to her feet in front of me, her hands slide the glasses off of my face to set them onto the table. "Only those who can understand the mysteries of the world can see you. The real you."

The crinkle in Finn's brows and the frown on his lips makes it clear that he isn't able to see the difference in my eye color. The gold. But Meg can. That's clear now too.

"Who are you? How can you know all of this?" My eyes examine her in suspicion. How can you see me?

"Your friend is filled with much doubt," Meg responds, answering the questions that reside only in my mind. "He does not understand this town's history, therefore he can not see the same as you do. Belief is a powerful weapon, Serelia. Be careful, especially of those you may trust." Her hand rests against mine, her warmth ensuring that I can believe her. "You can call me a friend or a guide. It's of no importance. I'm someone who is here for you. You always know where to find me. Now, it's time to find yourself."

Chapter 8

Finn drops me off at home after our encounter with Meg. Every inch of me is still tense with everything she said. Even when we got back to the car, the doubt in Finn's eyes as he surveyed my eyes, trying to see what Meg was talking about, but not saying anything as he likely saw the same green that has always been. But in the window behind him, the two bulbs of gold light shone back at me.

Before I'm able to walk out of Finn's car, he calls out and places his hand onto my arm. "Please don't tell me you believe what Meg said back there? It's nonsense, a myth conducted for little kids to scare them. You know that, right?"

I'm only able to nod as I know any verbal response won't match with such. Do you really know better? Do you not want to believe it's true just because it'd be easier then? None of this is easy. A part of me really does believe, but werewolves and magic? How?

Grandma sits on our weary couch as I walk inside, the television flashing some commercial across the static screen. "Hi, grandma," I place a kill onto her cheek and sit down opposite of her. "I'm sorry," the words breathe out of me. "I don't know how to explain it, but I needed to see Mom. I went to go see her."

A tear slips down as my conversation with her reenacts in my head, all of the spiteful words I said to her. "It's alright, sweetheart," Rose breathes a heavy sigh. "I'm just worried. I want to help you if you let me."

"Can you tell me about her?" The question stumbles out before I can think, knowing how much she hates discussing the past. She hasn't even mentioned my grandfather in years. But despite any struggle and debate in her mind, she speaks up.

"From what I've always known, your mother met your father in high school, not too much older than you are now. She started acting out and talking nonsense, all these impossible things. About a year later, she came home pregnant—with you." My lips suck inwards as she goes on. "I'm assuming she told your father and they fought about it, he was gone the next day with no trace. Even devastated, your mother's love for you never wavered. After you were born, your father came back one time to see your mother, but disappeared the same day once more. I never knew why. Abria tried to give you the perfect life until she couldn't anymore, and like I needed to make sure she was safe, I wanted to protect you as well."

A heaviness takes hold of my heart listening to grandma. My mother was hurt. She believed something so deeply it broke her sanity. My mother lost her life for me. Piece by piece she fell apart.

Placing her hand onto my cheek, her warmth sinking into my skin, she stands and goes to the kitchen to let me have a moment to myself. All of the stories I've been told today collide within me, fighting inside and causing a struggle for my lungs to receive any air. My body feels limp, on the verge of fainting, when the sound of branches breaking followed by heavy footsteps breaks me out of my stupor.

Walking over to the window, a shadow stands in the faint luminescence of the street light. The person tethered to it only a few feet from my house. Lapis blue eyes pierce through the window and onto me.

Join us.

The whisper entrances my body outside, my legs cooperating as they shuffle through the front door, yet my mind remains detached, aware. Keeping heedful as the shivers that inch down my spine warns me that any wrong move will result in misery. The whisper is one foreign to those I've heard before, and even with the darkened distance between us, each step tightens an invisible noose around my neck. An alarm in my mind ringing without pause. Something isn't right about this.

The moon's dull light outlines the shadow as I creep closer, yet every feature remains indistinctive as I walk. Fear boiling within and an ache throbbing through my limbs. A gamble for my life shuffling out in front of me, a dangerous game being played for when I finally reach the threatening being.

Right before I can approach them face-to-face, and like my more recent dreams, the figure shifts. A beast forms from the body of a person, a wolf now stands before me. And instead of the concealed features of their face, only their blue eyes glower at me.

Then it charges.

In a single breath, it closes the distance remaining between the two of us. Its lips rise into a snarl, a savage hunger reverberating through tightened fangs. Drawing backwards, my legs wobble as the ground beneath begins to shake. A scream that refuses to sound trapping the air inside.

Stumbling, I force my body to twist in the opposite direction, back towards my house. Run. That's all I can do. What I need to do to survive. Run.

Not one thought. Not one breath. Just one step prying off the ground after the other. Run.

A howl triumphs through the bones of the streets. A howl that beats against the air behind me. The sound pounds past my flesh and scratches an itch within my soul.

Every nerve in my body is on fire, the path around me blurs. Gravity becomes heavier with every stride, the odds of ever making it free against me.

It's playing a game with me. This wolf could have already killed me, but it's taunting me. I'm it's toy.

The burning pain spreads from my legs to the rest of my body, my chest scorching as the last remaining pants in my lungs huff out. But my home, my sanctuary of freedom, is so close in sight, only a few houses away. I need to keep running. I can make it. If I stop, even a slight hesitation, will surrender me to the fate inside of this wolf's jaws.

Then life reminds me that hope is a pipe dream for the chance of ever making it inside vanishes. Not by the wolf behind me, no, that's not what stops me. There's a second wolf.

Red and black eyes emerge ahead of me.

Surrounded by the nature of two maleficent wolves both behind me and in front, there isn't any other step or move I can make to escape. I halt, blue eyes and red eyes brimming closer and closer, bridging the distance from their prey—from me. These are my last moments.

My knees collide with the grass beneath. My eyes lock ahead in the empty space of night ahead, unbearing to look upon those eyes anymore. They can't be the last thing I see.

The battering of footsteps thump closer and from my peripheral vision I can see the blue-eyed wolf pounce, mouth agape as it leaps to deliver me to my death.

With one final breath, one final acceptance, my eyes track up to the sky above, meeting with the constellations that hang heavy tonight.

This is it, and my eyes close with the stars being the last thing I see.

But death never arrives. For the second time, I manage to avoid death despite its tight grasp at my throat.

Silence. No footsteps, no growling. I shiver as the air around me goes still. Everything is silent.

Was this all a hallucination? A delusion like the one my mother had so long ago?

When my eyes open, will this have all been some dark figment of my mind?

Though, before I can open my eyes to reveal what I hoped to be some delirium, all my questions are answered as the growling resumes in the distance.

As my eyelids flutter, the world blurring back into view after having squeezed my eyes shut so tightly, I can just make out the figures of the two wolves up ahead on the other side of the street.

When my sight clears, my gaze locks on the street ahead, a brutal brawl commencing between the two wolves. Dark silhouettes rustling amongst the lawn grass, the enchanting lambent of their eyes lucent against the dark of the night. The blue-eyed wolf ambushes the other wolf from behind, but the red-eyed wolf manages to match the attack and send the wolf back, landing underneath the faint light emitting from the street lamp.

You can't protect the girl forever. Her blood will be the next to spill. After yours.

The whispers hush as the austere voice of the blue-eyed wolf thunders through my mind. A heavy silence pursues in my head as the wolves continue to tear into one another. All there is left is the sound of the heavy thumps of the wolves bodies as they beat against the ground, the dirt and blades of grass crushing beneath their weight. The shredding of claws ripping into flesh, and their bright three-inch pale canines in a tight snarl, a guttural growl breathing between their clenched jaws.

The carmine of blood oozes under the warm light, painting the concrete red, as each wolf attempts to land that final bite. My body becomes stiff as the battle goes on, freezing me to my spot on the ground. I can't sit here waiting for my turn. But every muscle in my body is engulfed in a cold fear, unable to do anything but watch.

Watch as the two hunters encircle around one another, their eyes locked on the other. Shadows that tumble through the darkness. Untamed jaws open wide, merciless fangs starved for the taste of blood. Two beasts fighting the way soldiers do in war. Leave no enemy alive, only stopping when you're dead.

Now's my chance.

Rising up from the ground with a steady stillness, careful not to make any hasty movements as not to draw any attention onto myself, my eyes never break from the wolves ahead. As my back straightens out, I take one short step to the side. Please don't notice me. My lungs strain as I try to hold in my breath, but a quick gasp of air stutters out of my mouth as the wolves thrash against one another.

One foot after another, my steps begin to widen the further away I move from the fight. Tearing my eyes away from the wolves, I look behind me to see how far the safety of my house is. Two blocks down. You can make it.

Stepping up onto the curb, I hope the grass will muffle my footsteps as I begin to quicken the pace. Still walking backwards, my head bounces back and forth to keep my sight trained on the wolves while seeing how far the house is.

The silhouettes darken as the wolves tumble between the lawn and the separate street lights, but their eyes never dull no matter how far away I move. Just keep moving. Don't slow down now.

The red-eyed wolf surges forward, a quick bound for them to get the advantage over the other wolf. As the blue-eyed wolf attempts to recoil against the attack, the red-eyed wolf finds a weak spot and sends the wolf onto their side. As they press their front paws into the ribcage of the blue-eyed wolf, they inch their face down to theirs, teeth bared ready for the battle to be won.

Run. Now.

My hips twist as I turn to sprint the remainder of the way. I only get in one step, though, as my foot kicks a hidden sprinkler concealed in the tall grass.

Fuck. Please, don't let them hear me. My teeth grind together as I suppress the painful groan that burdens within my throat. Steadying my balance, I take a quick pause in hopes that the wolves are too far away to have heard anything, but as my gaze turns to the wolves, red-eyes peer onto me.

My breath hitches inside of my chest. There's no way I can make it back before the wolf catches me. There's a shiver that runs over my skin, sending chills through my blood, as I wait. And wait. But those red-eyes never move. The wolf only stares.

My head tilts slightly to the side, my sight interlocking with the wolf as in that moment, time wavers. Their eyes scan my own, as if the wolf is checking on me. Almost as if they are making sure I'm okay, dark eyes with a veil of... warmth? Steel-colored fur lights under the subtle light, making it undeniably clear that this is the wolf from my dreams. The wolf from the forest. The wolf my mother is so fearful of. Yet, all they do is stare.

Then there's a cry.

As both the wolf and I freeze in that second of time, the other wolf takes advantage of the distraction and digs their paw into the chest of the red-eyed wolf. The wolf falls, their side hitting the grass beneath and the blue-eyed wolf pounces upward. Sapphire eyes replacing the red as they now are the ones to peer deep into my own, only there's no warmth masking over them.

Leaving behind the red-eyed wolf bleeding out on the lawn, the wolf dives towards me. Its large nature makes the distant gap I made between us close in a few strides. Again, my feet are rooted to the ground below.

A harsh batter beats closer. The pumping of my heart strains as the black void of the wolf's mouth becomes all I can see. That and its sky eyes. All I can bear to think is why. Why does this wolf want me dead? The question burns along my tongue, wanting to shout it out as if the wolf would even answer.

Only a few feet away, the wolf quickens. But before its one last stride, there's a raucous whimper. Gray fur brushes across my vision, the red-eyed wolf surprising the wolf from the side as it knocks it off its lethal path.

Standing between the blue-eyed wolf and me, the wolf shields me from any further attack—proof that for whatever reason, they are my guardian.

The blue-eyed wolf takes a step forward, further challenging the wolf in their battle. Despite shaky balance, the red-eyed wolf doesn't stand down, but rather stands taller in defense.

Without advancing any further, those blue eyes halt where the wolf stands. There's nothing but silence and still air. Not a single whisper looming as if also awaiting the wolf's next move.

Their blue eyes shut closed, its head tilting up as their lips part in a crying howl at the moon. Then the wolf's gone. It vanishes into the darkness of the town's streets, leaving only me and one more.

Though the worry lingers of it turning around to kill me, the wolf only remains ahead. Its head turning back to look at me, its red eye illuminating under the moon's gleam. Worry within me dwindles as all I can do is marvel at the deadly beauty that stands in front of me. Those hints of recognition tying in with the security I can't help but feel with this wolf, that quiet voice inside telling me they're here to protect me at all costs.

It's an eternity of us staring at each other. The moon overtakes the both of us as it hovers just above. And soon enough, the wolf simply walks away. Leaving me here, sitting in complete awe at everything I've witnessed tonight.

Then all I can do is stare. Not into the distance, and not into the darkness. As the blue-eyed wolf had done before, my sight locks onto the moon above.

Chapter 9

Twenty feet of walking has never felt more like an eternity.

Hints of blood drop with each step onto the harsh concrete of the barren streets. My calf burns between each tooth-mark of where the wolf had bitten. I'm terrified that if I were to inspect it, a pound of flesh would be missing.

The darkness around burns red, a burdening reminder of the eyes I've been tormented by for so long. The growls of those wolves as they fought following me on my short journey, an anguish of what I faced moments ago.

My eyes cast down to the cracking pavement, the shadows of trees and houses being lit from the moon above. My mind wanders in Meg's tales, how I am a wolf. That this town was filled with werewolf-beings, that my father was one of them. How my mother is truly not insane, but rather the world is oblivious to the truth. That it can't be a mere coincidence that less than a day after these tales were spoken, I was attacked by such a creature.

Despite any faint yet lingering doubt, a new question brews. Is it possible the world I thought I knew for seventeen years is much more than I could have ever imagined? That perhaps the impossible is magical?

My questions are interrupted as I reach my house, my mind now filling with a plethora of excuses for grandma of where I had gone this time and explaining why I must look like I had been in a fight.

Though, as I open the door, I am not met with questions and lectures, but rather the fading smell of pasta and a living room that holds no life. Hobbling up the stairs, I realize I don't even know how long I've been gone for and grandma must have fallen asleep for the night.

Passing the door to enter my bedroom, I close it behind me and immediately go to take off my pants and take a glance at this bite. Blood oozes past hints of saliva through the bite mark, spilling down my leg and melting into the wooden floor. Well, I still have that pound of flesh, maybe an ounce instead.

Standing straight to go find a cloth to clean and wrap it, I balance my weight against the floor-length mirror in front of me. Leaning forward, I press my palm against the mirror, but instead of hard glass I am met with thin air and my body tilts forward to be met with dirt and twigs against my hand and knees.

"What the hell?" My eyes gaze upwards and focus only to find the forest surrounding me. How? Whispers creep down my ears, not the same whispers I've grown familiar with, but these ones are... chanting? They're saying my name over and over again as if it was a lullaby. A horror one at that.

Then there's only one.

The rest of the pack fades into the darkened trees, but one steps forward, inching closer until its eyes are directly parallel to mine. It's not the same wolf that attacked me earlier. Ruby eyes burn instead of sapphire blue. A fire tamed within the wolf's pupils, but it doesn't contain the bestial viciousness that flares behind them. It's impossible to tear my gaze away, despite the unsettling trembles that shudder within me. Its eyes are a more fierce weapon than any canine fang or claw, where a single glance leaves you lost in a reddened void of pure wrath.

White fur appears luminescent against such scorching eyes. A pure beauty that contrasts against eyes so hostile. Over the last few days, I've seen more wolves and have been attacked more times than what any sane person would consider normal. Ever since the wolves have emerged from the simple whispers in my mind, I've been attacked and hunted down by a number of them. Yet somehow, despite the fact that this wolf makes no movements of such, their presence holds much more power and ferity than any of the others.

Then the wolf speaks. A female voice rising above the now-silenced whispers. A voice so faint I'm unable to distinguish any unique qualities to define to whom it's belonging. Yet, despite its hushed words, it resonates through my mind until it conceals even my own thoughts.

You may have escaped, but I am not finished yet. The white wolf's eyes sparked as her words whispered against the echoes of the first. Her lowered voice surging within my brain. A throb of bitter cold grasping along the veins inside my body. Her presence urges a straining instinct within me to fight, but her words causing my mind to shrink within itself. Not until you have paid for the mistakes of you and your kind. There will be a time when protection is feeble and we will be ready. And you will fall, Serelia.

The wolf takes a step back, her eyes still interlocked with my own. She backs away, her white fur camouflaging with the darkness. The red of her eyes only burns brighter. The further she moves away, the arising impulses that rushes through me with a flood of adrenaline begin to calm. With the lack of her presence, my body begins to release from its strenuous distress. A swell of oxygen reaches my lungs. I hadn't noticed that I was holding my breath until there is relief as the air streams down my throat in a second gasp.

Rising up from the forest floor, the surrounding wolves replace her presence, creeping back into the light and encircling me.

Still I'm unsure if this is reality or a dream turned nightmare. Is it possible that the mirror led me to some other world, or is this haze merely another fantasy?

They inch forward, teeth bared and thick growls displacing the whispers. My head twists around my neck and the forest spins across my vision. The stars in the sky above now swirl between the trees and wolves, parading through my line of sight.

Their breath beats against my skin in a burning heat, yet their esurient teeth never touch and the forest around fades dark until there's nothing. Absolutely nothing.

I don't ever remember hitting the floor.

"Serelia!" Grandma's voice pierces the veil of emptiness inside of me. My eyes can only open enough to see her faces hovering above my own...

"Unresponsive..." a flutter of passing lights overhead, a crowd of blue masks surrounding. "Seventeen year old female found in a coma-like state according to grandmother, atrial fibrillation..." My conscious drifts off once more.

Another blaze of light attempts to fight the darkness, my body numb to the world except for the steady sound of beeping besides in a vacant hospital room. The light again loses...

And in the chasm of nothingness, a voice. "Alpha," his words echo in the void, words that cause a savage reaction of blood racing in my veins and sending goosebumps bursting along my skin. "Alpha, you need to hurry..."

Then I awaken.

A gasp of air freezes in my lungs, my body drowning in a sea of shadows. Being sucked down by the unseen waves of this abyss, falling down into nothing. Before ever reaching the bottom of what could lie at such a hole, my body forces upwards and lifts a hundred miles an hour up the unfilled vortex.

Everything stops.

"Hello?"

Am I dead?

"Where am I?" Though, despite how loud I scream, it's only me and the darkness. That is, until I hear him.

"Your own mind," he urges from in front of me, standing as if he's been there the entire time. It only takes one look into his eyes for recognition to take over. The boy, the one in my dreams... Caesar. "Your life is in danger. More so than it ever has been," he steps closer and his distant frame now towers over me. "It is time, Alpha. Come home."

His words don't register within my mind, ignoring his tone and instead asking, "What happened to me?"

"It's time for the dreams to stop and for you to awaken. Find us. Meet me at the edge of the woods, I'll find you when you do. And heed this, do not be followed." He pauses, his gaze branding his warnings into mine. "It is your time, Alpha."

Alpha...

The ground, or air, that was holding me steady vanishes from beneath me and I'm once more suffocating on the darkness. It's choking the life from my lungs and my brain goes weary, my eyes quivering until I can't hold my breath any longer.

It isn't until the pressure elevates from my body that I am able to draw in a heavy breath, the air warming the ice that filled my throat and body.

An unfamiliar woman stands over me, silenced words being spoken from her mouth to someone on my other side... Grandma, who jumps at the jolt of my body and sudden gasp for breath, panic and relief overwhelming her body in a swift moment.

The unfamiliar voice muffles in vibrations through my eyes until transforming into words blending with the tearful cries of grandma. "Miss. Lone, can you hear me?"

"Where am I?" The question croaks out of me, pushing my body and trying to gain focus on the room around me.

'The hospital, dear. Are you okay? What happened?" Grandma's answer rushes past her lips with the questions following as quickly.

"Wha- what happened to me?"

"Miss. Lone, my name is Dr. Wilson," she hesitates, deciding how to deliver what she needs to say next. "You have been in a coma for the past three days."

"What?" The single word whispers out in a struggling breath. Three days? "How? Can you tell me what happened?"

"We were hoping you could tell us what you know, your grandmother says she found you on your bedroom floor," Dr. Wilson describes, her voice completely neutral with each word as she speaks. "What do you remember?"

"I don't-" I stutter out, though everything that happened before the darkness is as clear as if it was still happening now. The wolf that attacked me, being saved by another one, falling into the mirror. Then being in that void, Caesar, everything he told me. Go to the woods.

"Serelia," Grandma speaks out now, "were you attacked? Is there anything you can tell us to help you?" But again, my voice can barely stumble out a letter, let alone a full answer.

"Miss. Lone, you have a substantial amount of scarring along your body. Can you tell us how you got those? Do you believe they have anything to do with what happened to you?"

The bite.

Throwing the thin blanket that stretched over my body, the paper-white hospital gown reveals my leg. Turning my calf over, expecting to see the blood still burning down my skin, I pause when I see it's gone. Or at least, almost gone. Rather than the gushing bite marks that sank deep into my leg, a faint scar rests upon the same place, almost fully healed.

"Miss. Lone?" The doctor questions, confused at my unex-pected movement. "Would it be best to speak in private? I am here to help you anyway I can." She continues, her mind possibly going to the idea of abuse or that I need to be examined for a padded cell.

"Um-" I try to come up with what to say. There's no way I can lie to a doctor, to be tested and inspected. I'd fail in a heartbeat and only find out that I'm certifiably insane. "No, I promise... Um, I need to go. I'll be okay, can I please leave?"

"Miss. Lone..."

I realize that if I rush out of here in a fury, they'll definitely want to keep me longer. So instead of lying, I put on an act. "I'm okay, truly. I just want to be in my own bed, I'm sure you can imagine it's been a lot for one day, or three I guess." The words ease past my lips now as I stand from the bed, my bare feet making contact with the chilled tile of the hospital. Playing on a gentle smile, I nod my head towards grandma, seeing if she will be able to help me out here.

From the doctor's suspicious eyes, I glance between her and grandma, a hint of hope flickering inside as I continue to charm and smile as innocently as possible for them to get out of this situation.

"Is she cleared to go home?" Grandma asks, a burst of relief flowing inside of me. "Can we go home, at least for now, and she comes back if needed? I think it's best, given her mot-..." She falters. "Given her past, it's be best for her if she can compose herself in her own space rather than here."

"Of course," Dr. Wilson nods, though her eyes still hint a bit of challenge behind them, questioning if this is a ploy for something else. Well, I guess it is. "I'll bring over her discharge papers and you'll be free to leave." She brings her stare back to me, "And Miss. Lone, if there's ever anything you may need, if you ever need help, please don't hesitate to reach out."

"Okay." Though, as I answer her, I know there is no help she or any hospital can offer for whatever that's happening to me. "Is it okay if I wait outside while she fills out the forms?"

Dr. Wilson hesitates for a moment, but nods in response. "I'll have them bring you a chair," she goes to call for someone, but I stop her.

"It's okay, I think it'll be good to put my legs to some use," and don't waste another second in changing into some clothes grandma had brought and walking out of this place.

"I guess it's true what they say," a familiar voice stops me as I pass one of the hospital corridors. The familiarity stinging worse than the wolf bite from last night.

Maeve.

"You really are your mother's daughter. I mean, of all places for me to find you. Well, isn't it perfect?" A wicked and mocking grin spreads across her face as she approaches, blocking my path to any sort of freedom. Her blue eyes filled with detest the closer she comes, though her stature lies smaller than my own, one look and she knows how much she can overpower someone, overpower me.

Maeve Sanchez is truly the perfect definition of beauty on the outside and beast within. Except, many fail to put down the mirrored veil she possesses and realize her true appearances. In all fairness, so did I for a long time.

"Though I can't say a hospital will help you much. Perhaps a zoo?" Her grin spreads wider and her tone stinging strong. "You know, awoo." A vicious laugh mixes with her howls, continuing to

"Why are you here, Maeve?" My teeth are gritted to where I think they'll shatter if there's even a hint of more pressure. It takes all the power I hold within me to stop myself from fighting back, from standing up to the girl who made the accident seem like hell's child's play compared to the misery she put me through.

"I volunteer here, living a life that is actually worthwhile. I know it's not a concept you would understand, right Lia?"

"You need to back off, I don't have time for this," I move to shove past her. As soon as my shoulder makes contact with hers, her hand reaches around mine and yanks me back in front of her.

"Who the hell do you think you are?" Spit flies out as she snarls. "I'm not done with you yet," her fingers dig into my arm, her nails almost sinking through my skin.

"I said back off," the burst of anger explodes from me as I yank my arm from hers.

"Look at you, all bark but still your tail remains between your legs. You are nothing, Serelia, understand that."

My eyes squint at her, the red fury in her eyes that seem almost unnatural. Like no one human eyes should look. No. The thought brings me back to the present. Paranoia is different from truth. This coma or whatever happened is screwing with your head. There's no way, of all people... Just no.

"It's easy for people to bleed, Serelia. Though, you would already know that," her finger brushes over the longer scar on my arm from the accident. A couple of nurses pass by the two of us and her grip relaxes on my arm, a plastered smile replacing her warped grin. Her voice chirps higher from her previous lowered tone, playing off our conversation as if we were friends. "I'll see you later," her grip releases from around my arm and she prances past me normally.

We're running out of time, Serelia. You need to find me. Caesar's voice rings in my ears, his warnings becoming more alarmed.

My body eases along the rest of the corridor before making it outside, then my body becomes limp. A puppet to an invisible master. My legs pull me forward, trekking through the streets and following a nonexistent map until after what feels like only a few minutes before coming to a halt. I'm here.

Come.

Chapter 10

The sound of something snapping from behind pauses me from questioning what Caesar meant. A branch crackles along with the rustling of leaves, followed by a pair of footsteps running. Though Caesar remains facing forward, completely still despite the intrusion, I turn to look for the intruder.

Nothing. Perhaps an animal? But the footsteps, they sounded too heavy. Glancing back to Caesar, his tall frame no longer stands besides me. He's gone.

How did he...?

But?

Searching around, I try to locate him in view knowing he couldn't' have gone far. He brought me here for a reason, there's no way he could have vanished. It's time. His words reverberated along my ears, though his lack of explanation leaves it as nothing more than another question in my mind.

Footsteps patter from behind me once more. Too loud to be any animal or tricks of the brain. This time I whip my body around to catch sight of who the being is, hoping to see Caesar, but once again, nothing.

Managing to find my way out of the woods, my trip home goes by rather briefly before another set of footsteps again stops me in my tracks along with the calling of my name.

"Serelia!" A voice from a distance shouts out, my eyes turning to make contact with Levana. Steadily meeting her halfway, she throws her arms around me in an embrace before continuing. "I've been looking for you, I haven't seen you in days. Please, I can't stand you being angry with me, I need you too much. I'm so sorry for what happened, just please..."

"Hey, I'm not mad. I'm sorry I haven't reached out, I've been... There's been a lot going on. I should have texted you back," I pull back and her arms loosen around.

"I thought you were still mad about what happened in the car, I promise I didn't mean for that to happen. I know how bad everything was for you, it won't ever happen again, I swear," she pauses and I nod at her, a silent gesture to accept her apologies.

I had honestly forgotten about the incident, everything has been happening so suddenly with Caesar and the coma. I know my panic must have made her think I was angry, but there was never any way I could stay mad at Levana. Not after how much she's helped me.

"It's okay, Levana. I'm not mad, I promise," and this time she nods in response.

"Are you okay? Where have you been?" She moves to my side and we begin walking along the concrete that connects to the town's park.

"Honestly, it's been a spiral of chaos and confusion," I say, keeping my gaze ahead and trying my best from having to explain it all. "How are you?"

She's silent for a moment, possibly debating on whether she believes me or not, but goes on as if she does. "Um... pretty busy, too," she rushes out in a single breath before perking up. "You know what the best medicine is for life... the mall!" She grabs my arms and drags me forward, rambling about the latest gossip and all the shops she wants to go to despite being 'a broke student,' all the way to the mall.

"What do you think?" I wiggle the current top in between my hands.

"Eh," Levana shrugs, "not your color. A bit too... eighties." She pulls the long-sleeve lime-colored top with the bell-like sleeves from my grip before shoving a burgundy lace corset top in replacement. "Try this one instead."

"For what? The clubs we're not allowed in?" I joke but still hold the top in front of my abdomen looking in the mirror. Grabbing the half-finished milkshake from the stool next to us, I sip the rest of the chocolate drink inside.

"Dude, are you drinking that or making out with it," Levana teases back and I flip her off while swallowing the last bit of it.

"I quite literally haven't eaten anything in days, sorry if I'm a little hungry," a snicker sounds from my mouth before setting the now-empty cup back down.

"Well I don't want to clean up that mess, and I'm sure neither do the workers here," she goes on, but passes me a couple of her leftover burger which I gladly accept.

Levana proceeds to drag me throughout the mall with bags slinging across both of our arms, indents marking deep into my skin from the weighted plastic. After a few hours of talking and shopping, and a quick car ride of our favorite songs, I now stand in front of my house fishing in one of the many bags for my keys.

Levana waves out of her window as I step inside, an over-whelming weight drains the energy right out of me as I walk into the room. No. I'm not ready. Having a few normal hours left me craving more. Needing more. My head is telling me to stay as far away as possible. From the forest and the calls that always whisper. From Caesar and his impossible riddles. Hell if I can stay awake forever to avoid another dream. Not having to worry about any dangers and wolves.

The whispers speak their hushed voices, but the more I tread into the living room, the more I can hear them. Hear him. The one voice louder than the others. He's here.

Despite the undeviating whispers, the house remains silent, all of the lights are off and any movement remains steady. But I know he's here. Somewhere.

With small and slow steps, one after the other, I check each room and try to maintain a sense of alarm.

I'm up here. Caesar says, a hint of amusement in his voice, though it registers in my head. This isn't some horror movie. Come upstairs. I'm tired of waiting.

Though I know he can sense me here, I tiptoe to the staircase and raise my foot to climb the first step, stopping myself before I could touch the ground. My stomach churns, the unknown of what awaits piling heavy on my chest. I want to release the long train of protests trapped in my throat, to erase all of my memories and thoughts and forget anything that has happened up until now. I should have ignored it from the very beginning, but these are the consequences of listening to the whispers.

No. It's time, as Caesar said. I need to come to terms that this is my life and that my life was never meant to be normal. That this is what needs to happen.

With a rustling sigh, I place my foot along the first step and climb up to my bedroom. My hand lies on the brass knob, the metal warm under my fingertips, and push open the door to what will inevitably be my fate.

Aside from a cool rush of air as I step inside, an open window which I know was not that way when I was last here, I take my stride into the empty room. With crickets chirping their soft son outside, the wooden floorboard creaks behind me, causing a sharp turn of my body back to face the door and there he stands.

Caesar. In the same clothes, his same eyes, same smirk.

"Took you long enough," he leans against my wall beside my mirror, his arms crossed and his eyes filled with levity. "Did you miss me?" His tone is one of arrogance, matched with his smug posture.

"Why are you here?" The words squeak from my mouth, a cringe immediately crosses my face and causes him to grin wider.

"We never finished our earlier chat," his voice is stoic as he speaks, mystery radiating from his presence.

"What chat? You said a total of four words."

His eyes show a quick flash of impress before shifting back to their neutral state. "It's time," he repeats himself from earlier.

"Not this again," I mutter. "Time for what?"

"Time you know the truth," his words trail out flat. "Who you are, the real you."

"I just want to be normal," my fingers fiddle amongst themselves and I peer down at the ground between us.

Caesar takes a step towards me, "Nothing about you is normal, Serelia." His closeness draws my eyes up to him, with only a bit more than a foot distancing his face from mine.

"So tell me," my head tilts awaiting his next response.

"Not here. We have to go to the place where it all started."

"And how do I know if I can trust you," I question, though I know I won't have any other choice. "That you won't kill me or something?"

His smirk again places on his lips, "If I wanted to kill you, why would I have saved you?" My eyebrows brush together in a furrow which leads him to going on. "I could have let that other wolf rip your throat out, but I didn't. I think that leaves some room for trust here."

His response doesn't ease me and he takes another step closer, his breath hot against my face and the smell of cinnamon and pine needles overwhelm my nose.

The smirk in his expression drops into seriousness, almost a silent plea. "You can trust me, Serelia. You know me. From that pretty little head of yours." His hand grabs ahold of mine, his fingers sending a spark in my own. His much larger hand is rough but gentle, making mine seem dainty in comparison. He tugs me to the mirror, the one I had fallen through the last time I was in this room. "Look into your eyes," he whispers in my ears as he stands behind me. The burning sun trapped in my eyes glows like orbs as they illuminate into the reflection. "Now touch the glass."

My palm reaches up once again onto the cold and flat surface. Immediately upon impact, the bedroom around me is replaced by a forest. Except this time, instead of being surrounded by malefic wolves, flowers bunch around my feet and there's a heavy scent of wet grass powering down my nose.

"You are a part of all this. You are nature. This, right here," Caesar shuffles beside me, his head tipping upward and watching the swaying leaves above. "This is your destiny. Your home. You need to accept this—this place, this life, in order to ever be able to accept yourself."

Taking in the evergreen trees that stretch on forever, my eyes flutter closed and I take a sharp inhale. Opening my eyes, I'm met with Caesar's intense ones and nod my head. "Okay."

"You need to believe, Serelia. I need you to believe."

The ferocity of his eyes sends shudders down my spine, his unwavering gaze never breaking.

"Believe in what?"

"Believe in me." His expression for the first time is guileless. No indication of arrogance or amusement, but sadness and pain, broken. The same eyes I've seen when I look in the mirror. There are no words that I can think of to respond, and instead give a slight nod.

"It's time," he says one more time, but this time, I know what he means.

Chapter 11

Separating my hand from the mirror, the thick, moonlit forest transforms back into my familiar and comforting bedroom.

"My eyes," the burning sun within them dims, fading until the gold shifts until they're once again forest green. "How?" How are they normal again?

"With the beginning of acceptance comes control. Your control over the wolf inside until you are no longer separate beings at odds, but one creature in complete unison," he pauses as I take in seeing myself in the mirror again. My normal self. "You have lived your life oblivious to the truth. A truth that everyone else refuses," Caesar speaks with a normal voice. "People have stopped believing in us. To them, we are fairy tales, but the wolves are real. The beasts are real. You are one of them."

My chest constricts as I hear his words, but locking eyes with Caesar's, his stare steadies my racing heart.

"How does no one know? How did I not know? All this time..."
I stammer, the words flowing out of me.

"You may have heard of 'werewolves,'" he begins and I nod.
"That's not what we are. We call ourselves Nocte Venandi, or
Night Hunters. Lupi works too. 'Night Hunters' is our particular
pack, but Lupi is what we are. For as bright as the moon shines,
the wolves shall shadow."

Spoken words fail, but my thoughts journey all across my
brain. And my mother knew about them? My father?

Caesar, as if reading my thoughts, responds. "Yes, your
mother knew. And yes, your father is one. That is why you can
never be normal. You are part Lupi and part human."

"Did my dad... is he?" My voice shakes as I speak. Is he dead?
My thoughts finish my question.

"No," Caesar answers in a swift moment. "Your father, Serelia, he is our Alpha. Our leader. He left only because it was his
duty, but his heart showed his true desires. Your mother. You.
Nonetheless, he did what he had to and now he is growing in
age. Soon the wolf will leave him and his reign will come to an
end. Because you are the daughter of an alpha, it is you who
must take his place."

"What does that mean?" I ask, trying to register what he tells
me. "The wolf is leaving him?"

"Quite literally as it sounds. The spirit of the wolf will no
longer reside in him. He won't have the power to continue
leading our pack. Though he can still transform, he won't have

the abilities to be a leader. And when he falls, so shall the rest of our pack. That is why it is up to you to save us. You are, or at least will be, our alpha."

Unable to process all of this information, more questions are all that I can form. "Meg, she mentioned a spell..." I trail off, narrowing my eyes at Caesar.

"Meg," Caesar lets out a soft simper. "Do you know she is one of the oldest of our kind? One of the originals of our pack in this town," he pauses. "She has been watching over you, Serelia, longer than you can ever imagine. You have never been alone. She is why no one has been able to harm you. Until now."

"How come now, then? Why are they getting close now, the other wolves?"

"For as long as she could, Meg has covered your scent," Caesar continues to answer my questions with ease, as if this was the most standard topic in the human race. Though, I guess if this is all true, he isn't human. "She made you appear as a mere human to any mystical beast so they were unable to locate you. Now, your transformation, it is unstoppable and that scent can no longer be concealed."

"The spell..." my words once again trail out unfinished. "She told me it prevented my transformation, but who placed it in the first place? My parents? Why? Why would they put it on me in the first place?" If it wasn't for Caesar placing his hands up to interrupt me, I would have spouted out the million other questions rummaging my brain.

"Take a breath, Doll. I don't know who placed the spell. If I am correct, your father once mentioned a witch, though I can't be sure. Though, I do know it was for you... so you can live a normal life, a perfect life, until the time came."

"Perfect life," I mumble. There has been no such thing as perfect for as long as I can remember. Guess we don't always get what we want, right dad? Ignoring the matter of my past, I ask the next question hanging at the tip of my tongue. "How did you visit me? In my dreams, I mean. Why do I hear these whispers everywhere I go?" I go on to ask more, but manage to stop myself so I can ensure I get all of the answers I need.

"Wolves are pack animals, as I'm sure you know. We howl at the moon as a signal. It's the same as that. You hear the other wolves, but because you are one, you hear their words rather than mere bellows. Our power intertwines us. In dreams, whispers, hearing what is said in the silence of our minds..." his eyebrows lift to confirm that he can indeed hear my thoughts. "They are all connected to the heart of being a wolf, of being in a pack."

"If my father never visited me, why did you? Why not him?"

"I can't speak for your father, but I do know all he wanted was to visit you. But if he did, because he is the alpha, he'd have put you at risk of being found. I visited because I was sent to protect you. Your mother did what she could to stop me, to prevent me from being near, so I did what I could. Your dreams," he stops before his playful smirk returns. "You must admit, though, you loved my visits. Didn't you?"

Rolling my eyes at his sudden liveliness, I ask the million dollar question that is the reason behind all of this. "So what's next? You told me to save you, save you from what?"

His smirk wipes from existence as his lips part. "A wolf, stronger than any of our kind has ever seen. One you have seen before." The blue-eyed wolf who attacked me. "No," Caesar breaks my thoughts, "that was a pup compared to what we are up against. Her minion. But she... she is so much more."

The white wolf. The one with the red eyes.

"Who- who is she?" Confusion fills my voice as my eyebrow lifts ever so slightly.

"That, we're unsure of. All we know is her motive. To eradicate our pack. To kill you. And to ensure that nothing will stop her from doing so." Though his words never waver, I can hear the fear inside of them. The same fear that shivers within me as he says them.

"How do you know it is a she then?" I falter out, wanting for this to be simply another dream. Maybe if I tried pinching myself-

A grin curls across Caesar's face, "please don't do that. I know how dire this all sounds, but it is real, I assure you that. The scent," he goes back to my previous question. "That's how we know it's a she. Once you finally shift, you will understand all that I tell you. But what is important is that you know everything, or at least all that you need to for now."

"What I don't understand is if you can't stop her, how do you expect me to?"

"Well that's why I am here, to help you tame the beast within and understand it. Only then, once you are ready, you will take over as alpha. Alpha's are the strongest and most valiant in any pack, that is how you will stop her." A shaky breath releases past my lips, but my eyes remain on his. "Serelia, you have always thought you were weak because you are different. In truth, you are the only one strong enough to help us. We need you."

Tears flood in my eyes, but I refuse to let them fall. My mother wasn't crazy. My father didn't abandon me, or not in the way I always believed. The whispers are real, they mean something. Everything I ever believed, about the world, my family, myself, it's all different now.

Caesar extends his hand and brushes my arm, his touch tingling against my skin. The stories, the dreams I have denied for so long. They're real. Not only are they real, but I stand within them. All the questions I've been asking all this time, or at least a part of them, I'm finally getting the answers I have been waiting for.

He gives me a moment, silent so I can process everything I've heard these last few minutes. Shutting my eyes, I hold back the tears that so desperately want to release. Though I can have my wishes of not having to leave or fight or face any of this, I know I have to. Apparently dreams are only made for sleeping.

Sucking in one more breath, I nod softly in acceptance. "I'm ready."

"Will I survive this," my pace slows as a nervous sigh breathes from my lips. "The fight, the pack... will I make it home?"

Caesar shifts my duffle bag in an awkward motion while I lug the other, traipsing through the hushed streets of Lupa Valley. After our conversation back in my bedroom, he helped me back my belongings into a couple of duffle bags and I left a note for grandma saying I'd be at Levana's. Then I texted her to cover for me before hiding my phone in my bedroom after Caesar informed me to in order to not be traced. Besides, it's not like enchanted werewolf forests have good wifi.

Though Caesar says it's only a bit past ten at night, the sky holds so much more darkness. The stars beam overhead, snow-white torches spread across a blackened canvas.

I look at him, still anticipating his response, but all I get is his eyes shadowed ahead and a clenched jaw. I guess he can't easily say, No, but that doesn't get you out of fighting for your pack.

"I wasn't going to say that," his voice reassures, causing me to freeze, still startled that he can hear what goes on inside my head. "I don't know what will happen, that's a fate no one can predict. All I know is we'll train you so that we can at least try to ensure the best outcome."

Pursing my lips tight, I bite down onto my tongue to hold in the anxiety forming. When that doesn't work, I change the subject. "You say you can hear my thoughts because you are a part of my pack," I begin and he nods in agreement. "Then why can't I hear yours?"

"As I've said, once you shift, this world and the life awaiting within will begin to make sense. That handy little spell placed upon you put a hold on your tricks, but once it wears off, your senses will surface." As he speaks, my feet begin to deceive me and my body trembles in fatigue the more we walk. Caesar must sense my weariness as he stops in his tracks, his nose twitching as he broods. "We can rest for the night, finish our journey in daylight."

"Where? We're too far from my house to go back, and we're not stashing hundreds in these bags for a hotel. Not that Lupa Valley has many of those either way," I say, glancing at the soundless road. Shop lights dulled for the night, only a few lone stragglers passing by. Caesar mentioned the forest being a bit more than a day's walk, and by now it's only been a bit longer than a few hours since leaving home.

"Perhaps not a hotel, but no one said the building had to be in use," Caesar eyes a few buildings down, his gaze landing on one covered in boards and fallen bricks.

"When I agreed to go with you, the deal didn't include breaking and entering," I try to sound bold, as if I had any say in what we did. But my voice fails me as the words break in my attempts.

"Would you prefer a tall tree or maybe a nice cave? I don't believe the rats and spiders will be welcoming company, however," he sneers in a sarcastic remark. My lack of protest must be enough of an answer for him as he begins to saunter towards the abandoned building.

It's for one night. I think as my eyelids are already near closed and it's a struggle to drag myself much further. We don't have many options regardless, at least this way you can sleep for a few moments.

In the midst of my thoughts, Caesar manages to find a few boards with a slight opening to them, with ease removing another two so we can climb in the already broken window.

"After you," he gestures towards the gap and despite a complaining groan, I comply.

Splintering wood pushes into my palms, not fully breaking the skin and sinking in, but still as painful. The hole is precisely wide enough to where I can climb through without much struggle, though I remain careful of any shattered glass and nails.

Nearly plummeting forward, I regain my balance and pretzel my body to land upright. From the moonlit town and graveled concrete, I now stand in what appears to be a darkened lobby with torn acrylic flooring and graying couches. Caesar lands besides me, his weight causing a thunderous echo across the large room. The lobby, clouded with a thick layer of dust, seems to have been part of an apartment complex that hasn't held a sign of life in decades.

"I guess this is what can be considered cheap real estate," I say while pushing against one of the longer couches, another wave of dust jumping from the cushion. The arenose of dirt particles wheezes a hoarse cough scratching against my throat.

The walls uncover what once looked to have been intricate murals, now reduced to faded paint colors and details now chipped to appear like abstract artistry. A whirring buzz of flies draws my eyes to a pot of brittle and decaying flowers, petals fusing to the archaic desk beneath that also holds aging light fixtures with bug-chewed base and lampshades.

Stepping away from the couch, I ascend up the thin staircase, the floorboards crying beneath my pressure. I'm met with a line of doors at the top, a few revealing bedrooms as forsaken as the lobby. Well, it's not five stars, but it is a place to sleep.

"We have only a few hours to rest, we should set back out before dawn strikes," Caesar approaches behind me, entering the bedroom and setting my bag on the wrinkled leather chair.

After a dozen attempts at dusting the bed off until I feel comfortable enough to lie down on it, I bunch up one of my hoodies as a makeshift pillow. In spite of how drained my body is, sinking into the mattress and rusted springs prodding against my sides, sleep does not come naturally tonight.

"I thought you were tired," Caesar mocks from the doorway, removing his jacket and placing it with my bags, exposing his muscular bare arms.

"I am," I grumble out, letting out a deep huff and shuffling for a more comfortable position in this bed. It squeaks as my body shifts and I fear it'll buckle if I were to move much more. "It's just- there's so much..." I try to explain but the words in my brain struggle to match with what comes out of my mouth. "I can't."

"It's okay to be scared, you know. Fear is what drives us to become stronger, without it, we can never push further as people," Caesar slides down the wall and sits on the floor opposite of my bedside.

"Okay, 'person,'" I say, bringing myself up to lean against my arms. "Tell me something about yourself. All I know about you is that you are a werewo-" I pause as his nose crunches at the word. "Lupi and that you have been dream-stalking me for years."

"Werewolves are monsters," he lectures. "We are hunters of the night. Far from mundane, sure, but monsters?" His head shakes as he pauses and exhales. "What do you want to know? I'll give you one question, anything you want to ask."

Struggling to think, the first thing I can think of blurts out before processing. "Tell me about your family," I begin stammering over my words, my voice lowering before finishing. "What were they like?"

Caesar's face flattens, all joking banter leaves his eyes as they close. "Not much to tell. Mother and father were killed when I was young, leaving me with a sister to raise as I searched for help. That's how I found the pack, your father. He rescued us. Raising us as his own for the next eleven years, ensuring our survival. My sister, Verena, is not much younger than you. She is my family."

Caesar's eyes, though looking in my direction, were unfocused as he spoke. A sadness on his face, one that I'm more than familiar with, and we both take a moment to sit in silence. We have both lost loved ones, family that were taken in ways beyond our control, and leaving us to fight life's harsh battles alone.

Though the two words 'I'm sorry,' nearly spill past my lips, I know more than anyone they're no help. Two words that sting rather than soothe.

"You should get some sleep," Caesar speaks out, keeping still in his position on the floor.

"Are you not tired?"

The woeful look on his face masks behind one of stone, a smirk hiding the grief in his eyes. "As you would say, 'werewolves' don't sleep much. Nights for us are spent running free, being nocturnal predators of the night. Soon you will join us, but for now, you remain more to your Maleo parts than the Virunis."

"Huh? What's that?" I ask, pulling my arms down from under me and lying my head back down onto my jacket, keeping my eyes on Caesar.

"Maleos are what we Virunis creatures call those who are mundane, human."

"So Virunis," the word doesn't flow as easily from my mouth as it does his. "Those are what, magical beings? Does that mean there's more than wolves?"

"All those tales you've heard in stories are true. Over time, Maleos lost their belief in us and saw us as monsters or legends. Though, it is the Maleos who have acted the most cruel than any Virunus being, so we went into hiding. Fatals, Lupi, Divines, Lamias— all of the creatures who conceal their existence beneath the moon's graces. I'll explain it all when the time comes, but for now, regain your strength, we must leave soon."

Chapter 12

Before my eyes shut fully for the night, they open once more quickly to look at Caesar. "You won't transform and kill me, will you?" A laugh follows my question, but the thought does cross my mind.

His shoulders fall with another exhale. "Why do you constantly question me killing you, Doll? Get some sleep, I beg."

My body eventually gives into the exhaustion, a dream flooding into my mind. This time, however, it is not the forest that comes.

I'm at home.

Standing on the outside in front of my house, a woman walks out the front door.

"Mom?"

It can't be. She looks... young. Her eyes beam with happiness and love, a smile unfurling on her pink lips. A blood-red dress drapes off her figure, flowing with the autumn breeze and strappy brown sandals to match peeking beneath. Her hickory-colored hair loosely dangles in a braid, swaying down her back.

No. It's not her.

"Abria!" the woman shouts with glee. A little girl runs out from behind me. A bright green top hiding beneath dirt-covered overalls, white shoes even more muddied, and pigtails flopping against her shoulders.

"Mommy!" the girl runs into the woman's arms. Into grandma's arms. "I saw my friend! He came to me again!"

A breath catches inside of my throat. That's her. My mother.

She's so innocent. Pure. Happy... Sane. Something I haven't seen in her for so long.

They don't take any notice of me as they continue talking. "Oh, did he now?"

"He told me stories," Abria shouts with child-free delight. She can't be more than five or six years old. "About the wolves and how in the sun they look like us!" Energy beams with her every word.

"Just be careful, darling," skepticism flows with grandma as she speaks, drawing this out to possible childish imagination. Little does she realize...

The dream around me ripples, changing.

The setting around me flashes forward, the scene around me aging as if the world was put on accelerating speeds before shifting altogether. The house vanishes followed by mom and grandma, changing until I stand at the treeline of the woods.

This time, a girl my age runs towards the edge between the open space and the dense trees, stopping only a few feet from me. With a red flannel hugging her waist, matched with snow colored shorts and a gray top to match. So easily and naturally beautiful.

"Aryce," she shouts out. It's her again, mom. Only older this time. She's calling for my father.

A boy materializes deep beyond in the woods to where we stand. Green eyes overflowing with worry as he races to my mother.

"Abria," he wraps her into his arms. Though time has sped up, both have such a youthful glow in their presence. They can't be much older than me here. "What's happened?"

My mother's eyes flicker with love as he sets her down and her teeth radiate with her smile. "I'm pregnant," her hands cover her small stomach as the words pass her lips in an exhilarating whisper.

As soon as he registers the words, my father matches my mother's smile, his lips touching both ears as he picks her up in his arms. The two of them twirl in joy before he sets her down and places a gentle but passionate kiss on her lips. When did everything change? Grandma said he had left the day after, what happened?

Before they can say anything further, the scene once more changes. But this time, I'm alone. Rain cascades around me, striking my skin yet somehow I remain absolutely dry. I'm in a much more secluded and foggy part deep in the forest. Only the sound of rain pummeling the tree's leaves can be heard.

Taking a single step, my foot splashes amongst a puddle, shallow enough that I can continue forward. Venturing to be able to figure out where I am, all that is around me is casted in darkness. Step after step until I try running, the puddle remains endless.

The water splashes high around me when I concede in defeat, finding my reflection in the mirrored water along my knees. Yet it is not my reflection that I see. Or at least, not fully.

Half of my face conveys as normal in the reflection, human. Even my eye glares its green color again. But the other half... I'm a wolf.

With its sun-shining eye that glows in the inky waters, a brown wolf makes up what should be the other half of my face. The water begins to move, waves wading as if a force was stomping along it. Then the water stops, freezing at once until it begins to crack along my reflection. Pieces of me sinking inside the boundless puddle, chipping away until there's nothing left.

A gasp hauls out of my lungs as the water pulls me under, submerging me down below where I'm unable to move. Water leaks into my body, drowning me from the inside.

Deep below, only a pure blue filling the space around. I can feel the force of my legs attempting to kick below me, straining against the water's crushing control. The sound of the blood being pumped in my heart's chest begins to ease, soon to stop completely.

Then, there's peace. Even in a moment so terrifying, knowing I am about to die, I find peace.

Bubbles form around me as I give my final breaths. The fight within me ceases as my legs stop in their attempts to swim upwards. I allow the wintry waters to sink my body lower in this chasm of water, a readiness for what comes next washing over me.

Closing my eyes, I allow myself to die.

"Serelia!"

My body thrusts forward as an arduous breath fills my lungs. Taking in the air as fast as a hungry person dines at a buffet. Even after, my breathing comes unsteady and I draw my hand up from my chest to my dampened face.

"Serelia," Caesar rushes to my side, pressing his hand against my back and helping to lift me up. "What did you see?"

I try to steady my words, but can barely let out a tensing breath without choking. "My mother..." the words retch out in a struggle. "Her memories..."

My body trembles beneath Caesar's touch, tears spill unwillingly from my eyes as I peer into his. The world around me slows as the rapidness of my heart batters inside of my chest. I attempt to swallow down the rising flood in my throat, my body still drowning despite me now being awake. My lungs are burning for fresh air, but with each inhale enters another surge of the water as if I was still underwater.

Caesar wraps my body within his own, a tight embrace bringing me up to the surface. His warmth acts as a shield against the darkness that tries to consume me, a stillness washing over and calming my breathing. His chest slows and a faint shush surrounds the air around me, reassuring whispers brushing against my forehead.

"I'm here, you're safe, Doll. Feel my breaths. I promise, I won't let you fall."

His words barely reach my ears before I drift off engulfed in his serene warmth that starts to melt the remaining darkness within.

The creaking of a door opening startles me awake, my eyes opening to a dimly lit room and specks of dust floating over my head.

"Finally. I spent an hour trying to wake you. Did you know you snore, Doll?"

"I don't," I protest, swinging my legs over the bed and sitting up at the edge. Caesar moves further into the bedroom, tossing a plastic bag onto the mattress beside me. My eyes scan over the bag before looking back to Caesar, my eyebrow raising in question.

"Lunch time," he says, opening the bag and pulling out a plastic container, the clear lid revealing a stack of pancakes and eggs. "We still have a bit of ways before we reach the forest, gather your strength before we leave."

My head tilts towards the pancakes, my eyebrow still raised inquiring where the food had come from. It's not like this old apartment has free food services. "Where-"

His hand raises, stopping me from finishing my question. "Let's just say some sap may be a tad pissed off when his order isn't there for pickup."

"But whe-" I begin to start again, but pause before I can say anymore. "Nevermind, I don't care."

My body flops back down onto the mattress beneath me, tugging my sweater under my head, pressing it against my face in hopes of more sleep.

"No, no," footsteps draw near before my sweater is pried from my hands. "We can't waste anymore daylight. I already let you sleep in, but nothing about this journey will be easy should we wait until nightfall."

With a fussing groan, I force my body back upwards, a muttering of complaints objecting under my breath. Picking up one of my duffel bags from the doorway and setting it on top of the bed, I take out a few fresh clothes to change into.

Sensing Caesar's presence remaining behind, I twirl my head around to catch sight of him. "A little privacy?"

"If you insist," a smirk plays upon his face as he walks out of the room, shutting the door behind him.

Changing out of my worn clothes and into the fresh ones, I peer into the spotty mirror in the corner of the room. Ugh, what I would give for a shower. My eyes flickering between some of the grimier spots along the glass.

Everything is about to change. It already has in a single night. What else is going to happen when we get to the forest? My father—will I even be able to face him? Hell, seeing my father is going to be the least of my concerns when we get there.

How the hell am I going to do this?

A knock at the door snaps me from the anxiety that is building within. "Serelia, are you okay?"

"I'm fine," pulling away from the mirror and opening the door to Caesar standing on the other side. "What are we waiting for? Let's go."

After 'checking-out' of our little stay, basically sneaking back through the boarded window we had come through in the first place, Caesar and I headed back towards the main road. Continuing our travels towards the forest, the streets now awaken with the dawn's light.

People going out to breakfasts at the diners, others making their way for a day of work. Children filling in school buses on their way to school, a few individuals strolling in a morning jog.

"Serelia?" A voice startles from behind, quickening steps nearing behind Caesar and me. No one can know that I'm leaving or why. As their steps draw closer to me, I whip my body around to catch sight of the caller only a few feet from where I stand.

"Finn? Why are you-"

"What?" He interrupts, his head trailing across my face and down to my duffel bag before moving to Caesar. "What are you doing here? Who is this?"

"It's none of your business, Finn," I reply, attempting to make my voice as carefree to avoid suspicions. "Just leave me alone, please."

"No," Finn declares, still glancing back and forth between Caesar and me. "Are you okay, Serelia? Who is this?" His voice grows more demanding, concern lining along as he speaks.

"The guy from her dreams," Caesar chirps before I have a chance to respond, his playful smirk now smug and teasing as he glares at Finn. My elbow nudges into his side as I take note of Finn's uneasy reaction, a grunt following as I make contact with his ribs.

"Serelia, can we talk? Alone." Finn urges, his hand reaching out for mine which I avoid.

"There's nothing to discuss, Finn."

"Serelia, it's time we go," Caesar's voice drops into a firm tone, a silent reminder of the gravity of what we have to do. What we're here for in the first place.

"Don't, Serelia. I can help you, just talk to me," his hand this time wraps around my arm, tugging slightly to pull me away from Caesar.

Jerking my arm out of Finn's clasp, I scowl. "I said there's nothing to talk about, Finn. Seriously, leave me alone." I emphasize those last words before turning my back on him, trudging forward with Caesar striding next to me.

"It's clear there's some history there," Caesar attempts to lighten the tension as we saunter away. "What was that about?"

"Nothing important," I murmur.

As the edge of the woods comes into view, I gaze over to the side. The vision of my mother and father replaying out in front of me as if they were still there.

"Are you ready, Doll? You know there's no going back once we reach the forest."

This is it. Once I cross these borders, the life I knew will never be the same. Nothing ever will be again. I may not even come out. The future and how fast it's coming is so unclear, but it's a risk I have no choice but to take. The person I am, who I was, she will be gone. For good.

"For as bright as the moon shines, right?" I say, proceeding to the forest for what may be the last time. Never looking back at the city behind me and what may be my last few moments in the human world.

Chapter 13

Silence overcomes the forest as the immense green entraps me, the light peeking through the slight separation of leaves. A small echo of breeze and grass shuffling whirs in my ears, the wind brushes against my skin, and a scent of moss fills my nose. The scenery is limitless as plants dance and drops of gold pierce through broken leaves above. Butterflies with blue wings shine across the shadows, irradiating the branches as their movements flow on the vines of trees. Nearby are the roars of a waterfall, drumming against the ground and vibrating the land where I tread.

A spongy air full of heat and dampness creates a light sweat that prickles along my forehead and arms. Humidity frizzes my hair and my clothes stick to my body the further we travel.

A sense of home filling the fear I once felt among this forest, the trembling cold that frightened me when I visited here in my dreams. Though, past the verdant trees of the forest, I recognize how far from simple dreams and nightmares this place is now as I venture further into this cervix of infinite woods that no human has ever known to exist.

"Do you feel that, Doll?" Caesar's breath flutters besides my ear. "This is who you are. You have always felt that you never fit in. But that's because that town, that life, is not your home... This is. You are a part of what makes this, all of this, beautiful," he pauses, stepping around me and taking a hold of my hand. His touch sends a ripple of tingles up my arm, butterfly wings grazing my skin. "Tell me what you see."

"Everything... It looks like it's glowing. All of it." Colors so coruscating, blending and mixing yet each shade stands out as much as the other, I couldn't even name each one. I can't help but take note of how every branch curves and how each blade stands tall. The beautiful melody of the birds as they chirp from the towering trees that emanate evergreen and mocha.

"Do you feel that prickle amidst your bones? The quickening of your heart? A sudden impulse to run and never stop?" He pauses, though I remain quiet while my senses overwhelm. "Soon, very soon, you will become a full Lupi. Soon you will understand not only what it means to be a Lupi, but a Virunis."

"When will I know it's time?" My eyes dance through the forest, unable to avert them from the beauty in front of me.

"That is the decision of the moon. And you, the more you begin to accept this life, the easier it will be for you to overpower the spell. Hopefully, bringing you back brings some speed to that process."

"When was yours?" My gaze breaks from the trees and I turn my head to Caesar who stands right behind. "Your first transformation?"

A display of remembrance flashes through his eyes. My life as a Lupi has barely begun, but for him... for Caesar, this has been the only life he's known. "Eleven years ago. I had only just turned eight. My parents were considered strays, wolves who had no pack aside from each other plus my sister and I. Regardless, I have ran with the wolves for the majority of my life just as the wolf has ran within me."

Before he or I could say anything more, a low growl cuts off any further response.

The next few moments happen too quickly.

Caesar grabs my hand, twisting my body to now fully face him. My head tilts up, his red and black eyes flaring against the darkness. His grip tense against mine, his stance firm in a shield of defense. Footsteps near. Multiple footsteps surrounding all around.

"It's a shame the wolf will never run within you, Serelia," a heavy voice draws from my right side. A wolf approaching from between the trees. Dark brown fur brightened by an amber eye. His other eye is achromatic white, a deep scar tracing deep across from the lining of his ear, to the beginning of his nose. Caesar pulls me around until all that is in view is his leather jacket, his muscles tense inside the fabric.

"Stay behind me," he hisses, though his tone is clearly directed towards the wolf ahead rather than me. His arm wraps around his back, my hands clutching onto his forearm. His body hardened, his stare never wavering or breaking from the intruding wolf. Under his growl, the name, "Cicatrix" spits under his breath.

Other wolves begin to entrap us. Each one snarling with canines craving the taste of blood. Ready to pounce at the first chance they get.

"You can't protect her, Herou. You know she has been looking for the girl." The wolf Caesar called Cicatrix says, his words cold, matching the sharp air of the forest. The wolf who Caesar warned me about. The 'she' that even he seems to be so afraid of. Someone stronger than even the oldest of their pack has ever seen.

The wolf charges. From one blink to the next, Caesar shifts from man to wolf. His leather jacket shifting into ash gray fur before he and the other wolf lunge at each other. The rest rushing towards me. Picking up a fallen branch, in my best efforts at protecting myself, I swing.

Growls echo within the clearing as Caesar and the other wolf charge. Eight wolves attempting to subdue me. A wailing cry bouncing off the trees. Caesar and Cicatrix continue to restrain the other. Rolling and trashing against the humid dirt, flinging the other around. Tearing into each other's limbs, sharp claws ripping out pieces of fur and flesh. Blood trickling from their nails and jaws, sinking into the ground.

One of the wolves manages to pull the branch from my grasp. The rigid edges shredding my palms. A penetrating shriek tears its way from my throat, scratching against my vocal chords, threatening to rip them apart. A second wolf taking the opportunity to immobilize me. My back pinned against the ground, his paws pressing against my shoulders. Drool oozing onto my face from the fangs lingering over me.

"Serelia," Caesar's voice overwhelms the growling overhead and the sounds of my own screams. My neck twists in time to see his eyes shifting onto me, the fierceness held within them fading into fear. Just one second. One moment of distraction. The next he is bound against the soil.

No!

A scream tears through swollen vocal chords, and before the echoes can fade from existence, Cicatrix subdues Caesar and sinks his claws down. A cry shocks the forest around. One so aching, it draws me back to the night of the accident, the screams my mother released right before...

Dark blood gushes from Caesar's neck, drenching his fur as Cicatrix continues to tear his flesh. His body goes limp against the dirt as Cicatrix pulls his paw back for a final blow.

Help him. Transform. Move. Something. I need to save him. I can't let him die.

I struggle beneath the wolf on top of me. His paw pinning down against my neck, claws nearly piercing into my throat. My veins throb against my skin about to burst as life starts to be choked out of me. A mixture of blood and drool dripping down my neck. A lacerating and searing pain numbed as I can only focus on the trickling running along my skin.

My eyeballs pulsate and start to roll back, a pressure holding any last breaths within my straining lungs, unable to allow them free. I close them ready for my end. The last thing to ever be seen is the burning eyes of the wolf above.

A howl resounds before a sudden breeze.

Before the wolf above can strike their final blow to end my life, another howl wails out, followed by the staggering beat of running in the short distance. Multiple steps quickening, slapping the muddied grounds. Branches snap and leaves crumble beneath the weight. Footsteps moving closer and closer. Nearing until the sight of wolves appears all around. So many wolves. All snarling as they race towards us, nearly thirty wolves causing a commotion of a stampede filled with hundreds. Yet still, the question beats against my fainting heart. Are they here to help us, or kill us? But that small grain of hope keeps these last breaths of mine going, holding out for as long as I possibly can until I know for sure.

Another howl bays closer.

One by one, more wolves continue to near. Leading the pack is a smaller wolf, but filled with so much aggression.

As the wolves stride closer, I see the fury within the leader's comet-blue eyes, a light gray fur that beats against the proud creature. Their eyes shift from myself and the attacking wolves, to Cicatrix and Caesar still beneath him. With that one look of Caesar's near-motionless body, anger blazes to hysteria.

"Caesar," a female's voice whispers from the leading wolf, a demanding tone laced with wrath the closer the approaches. Another howl releases into the crisp air as the rest of the wolves come into view, encircling around us. They charge and begin to separate, the majority of them beginning to attack the wolves closest to me. The others, including the lead wolf, go for Caesar.

Caesar.

His weak cries muffle out the snarls. He's calling out for me. His words are broken by the soft whisper of groans heavy breaths. Despite the evident pain that lines his cries, I know it is not one that is looking for help. No. He's still trying to protect me. Trying to get to me. Even when I can't do anything in return to help him— to save him.

And despite how desperately I want to look away, unable to see him in this amount of pain, I keep my eyes on his as he struggles to get up. Cicatrix still remains on top of him, his body covered in soaking blood and the claw marks pouring any blood left.

Weariness begins to take over my last existing breaths and the remaining strength that is keeping me awake. The fact that

I am not dead after yet, after everything that has happened so far, is that force that reminds me to keep fighting.

The wolf still over me focuses back down, a hunger stirring in their eyes as their face draws closer to mine. They're not going to make it in time. This is it. Sadness resides in my dying heart, my blood starting to run cold, and all I could think of is Caesar. How I can still hear his cries. How those cries will be the last thing I ever hear. Misery and regret will be the last thing I ever feel. Regret how I couldn't help save him, save his pack, after all.

This is it.

But before the wolf's hunger could be satisfied, a wolf springs forward and collides their paw with his neck, restraining him to the ground in the same position he had over me. A sudden breath forces itself down into my lungs, almost choking on air as I take a dense inhale with eager lungs welcoming in each gasp. With one swipe of their paw, the wolf's blood splatters, killing him in less than a second.

Sitting up, my gaze moves back towards Caesar to see the leading, small wolf now challenging Cicatrix. Caesar, though, his attention remains on me, struggling the same fight I did to stay alive. And if I'm alive, that means he can survive this too.

"There are more of us," Cicatrix's voice bellows out, defensive against the wolf, but his eyes landing on me as his words ring out. "There will always be more. And soon, she will come for you."

Without the wasting of another moment, the female wolf stampedes towards Cicatrix, closing any remaining distance between them.

"For my brother," the female's voice bellows before she stampedes towards Cicatrix, closing the distance between the two.

As she springs forwards, her claws outstretched, ready to sink down into Cicatrix. Though, he is ready for her attack. He dodges her body, managing to side swipe her ribs and draw a light blood that sprinkles onto the ground. Two other wolves follow her, attempting to attack Cicatrix at once, but despite the three-on-one, all three wolves are tiny compared to him. Cicatrix takes down one of the wolves, then the other. Doing so without any major injuries to himself. With ease, he scratches at their faces, claw marks tearing the skin from one wolf's ear down to their neck before plunging into the second wolf, ripping out a larger chunk of his neck.

He's too strong. They won't be able to stop him.

The female wolf strikes once more from behind. As she finally manages to spill some of Cicatrix's blood for the first time, a small ounce of hope glistens within that they can overpower him. Hope that in a blink is burned to nothing as he spins and pins himself over her. The female wolf snipes at Cicatrix, but despite her efforts, she is unable to move from beneath his weight. His face inches from hers, clenched fangs that through them releases a growl so taunting it sounds like a laugh. Ready to end her life the way a child tears up a dry twig.

But her fate never approaches. One of the gray wolves beside her brings themself off the ground and tackling Cicatrix from the side when he is distracted on the female. The gray wolf, despite being smaller, finds a footing over Cicatrix as the female wolf and the other one who attacked alongside them constrain him.

"It's over, Cicatrix," the female wolf delivers a carnivorous snarl, inching from Cicatrix's face as he did hers. Her words are determined as her front paw rises, a weapon drawn and ready to kill the wolf beneath her.

Desperation, for only one moment, floods Cicatrix's eyes. There is no more escape. No more moves to be made. This is it for him.

Only it isn't.

He finds one last move he can make.

His jaw widens, exposing his red-tipped canines, and bites down on the neck of the gray wolf that stands over him. An instant, excruciating wail echoes through the forest. The gray wolf collapses off of Cicatrix, allowing him the opportunity to rise up from the ground, sprinting off in the following seconds.

He's gone.

Chapter 14

"Lowell," the female wolf cries out to the wolf beside her as their body remains on the ground. Though, I drown them out and shift my sights elsewhere.

"Caesar," his name bawls out past my lips. Finally, I lift my body up from the ground and run to him. Still in his wolf form, his body remains limp. Blood swirling between his fur, soaking into the dirt that sponges it up. My hand hovers over the holes that mark his skin, debating if it's worth it to stop the bleeding. I hesitate, fearful that by touching him I'll hurt him even further. Instead, my hand lands onto his head, tracing over the side of his face. As my skin presses against his soft fur, looking for any indication of breathing— any signs of life. Nothing. Instead, it's almost as if his pain transfers through my touch. My eyes shut in a wince, tears forming within my eyes, as I replay him jumping in front of me when the wolves attacked. How I'm the reason for his suffering.

Please don't die. Please.

My face drops down close to his, a whispered breath pleading for him to wake up. "I'm so sorry," my voice strains out. Words so quiet, I'm not a hundred percent sure they came out at all. Still, I continue, "I couldn't help you. I couldn't protect you like you did for me. But I'm not giving up on you. Keep fighting, please."

A small movement twitches beneath my fingertips. Guiding my head back upwards, I look for another movement, wondering if I purely imagined it. But the short and faint movements of Caesar's chest rising and falling confirms what my eyes are seeing. He's alive.

A rush of comfort and relief engulfs me. More so when his eyes briefly flutter open. The red and black of his irises flickering before his eyes shut once again.

"Caesar, stay awake. Please, wake up. You need to keep your eyes open," fear collides with guilt as he's unable to open his eyes once more. His body begins to tremble and his breaths become lighter. He's fighting. Despite all of the pain he's in, he's fighting.

"We'll save him," a woman's voice shocks me from behind. Twisting my head, the sight of a human girl stands close to me. "Both of them," she says, despair lining her voice, as she looks off to the side where a few other people surround the gray wolf who was bitten. Bringing her gaze back onto me, she kneels down to become eye-level with me. "You must be Serelia," she pauses, her eyes sweeping across my face. "Caesar did always say you looked like Abria. I can finally see the resemblance."

My eyes cast downwards, the shame leaving another painful wound at the thought of my last interaction with her. The guilt of my mother being locked up even though she truly isn't insane, but rather living in a truth others are too ignorant to believe. Being called mad by all of society—by me.

"I'm Verena," the girl goes on. "I apologize for anything my brother may have said or done prior to catching up with us," she lets off a doleful smile as her sight lands on Caesar.

"You're Verena? His sister-" I trail off, remembering what Caesar had told me about his past.

"So I take it that he's mentioned me?" Her soft smile widens. "Yes," she nods in confirmation while going on, "and anything he's said about me is untrue. I'm a much better fighter than him." A warmth fills Verena's voice as she speaks, but as she takes a second, her smile falls and her words rush out quicker. "We need to go. A Lupi bite is not a wound so easily healed. Lowell and Caesar, they both need to be healed before it's too late."

As she stands upright, the family resemblance between her and Caesar is evident. Her long, dark hair cascades down her shoulders, a deep color almost the color of charcoal. Brown eyes as piercing as Caesar's, only a bit darker in shade.

By the time I look around to gain a sense of my surroundings, the majority of the wolves have shifted back into human form.

Some of them approach Caesar and I as I still sit next to him, crowding around Caesar before lifting him up. Some of the others in human form do the same for Lowell while the rest who remain in wolf form shape into a defensive line like guards.

"One of our own will run ahead to notify our healer for our return. We mustn't waste anymore time," one of the men carrying Caesar says to Verena and I.

All of the wolves and humans move out of the clearing where the attack happened. I follow alongside Verena and the people that are carrying Caesar as we move to continue our ascension deeper into the forest.

"Those wolves back there," my voice breaks the silence while noticing the distinct concern etched along her face. "They're helping the wolf that Caesar warned me about, right? The ones who want to harm your pack?"

"Our pack," Verena corrects me, though the thought of me being a part of this pack is still a fact I have yet to fully come to terms with yet. "Children of the Crimson Moon," she continues on. "I assume Caesar told you about us, the Nocte Venandi, yes? Well you're right, this pack, the Crimson Children, are dedicated to hunting our kind and any other packs that follow the Virunis order. Their leader, the one you've been warned about... She is willing to do anything to ensure that all Lupi fall beneath her—especially ours.

"Why yours especially?"

"No one knows for sure. It's been a war that's played out for decades, but the Crimson Children have strengthened. In numbers, in power. We worry that these battles will come to an end soon enough. Ending with us burning to ashes as the Crimson Children rise to power. That is why we have come for you now."

"I still don't understand how you all think I can help. I'm not a warrior or a fighter like the rest of you. I couldn't even transform to save Caesar back there," the guilt returns and my eyes draw down remembering how I failed him. That Caesar could have died back there. That he still can.

"Hey," Verena grabs onto my upper arm and halts me in my steps. "You never learned about this world the same way we have. You can't blame yourself for that. It's all going to take some time, and we're all here to help you adjust. It's not easy to take in all at once."

"I don't think I'll ever be able to take in how only a few days ago my biggest concern was surviving high school and the idea that I was going insane. Now, I simply have to survive."

"And I know it's going to take more than some pep talk where I tell you it's best if you accept yourself as a Lupi and your fate as an Alpha," her hand places on top of my shoulder with sympathetic eyes looking into mine. "Look, Serelia. Your whole life has already changed so much, and it's going to keep changing. But remember, this is what you were born to do. Soon, your instincts will take control and you won't even realize how much you fit in with us. No matter what you think, you are strong enough for this. This life. You are a Lupi."

"It doesn't feel that way," a heavy sigh exhales through my nose.

"It will," Verena smiles, a silent reassurance.

"And until then, all we have to do is what? Save both Caesar and Lowell, then figure out a plan to stop what I've been told is the most vicious she-wolf being before she kills the entire pack and apparently overpowers the rest of Virunis life."

"Seems about right, should be easy enough," her sarcasm causes the both of us to laugh briefly before she speaks again. "I can see why my brother has been so fascinated by you all of these years. He's never once hesitated in a fight, for anyone."

"Well he's lucky you arrived when you did. We both are," I tilt my head to look back at him still unconscious. On the other side of him, Lowell is being carried. The bite mark on his neck is visible from where I walk. "A wolf's bite, why is it different from any other injury?" I remember back to when I was bitten by the wolf, when Caesar saved me. "I was bitten, why is Lowell more affected than I was?"

"When the war broke out between the Virunis creatures, the Divines placed a spell on the bite of a Lupi for our beings to be the fiercest warriors. But for this ability, there was also a deal. As long as we bring no harm to them, but rather protection, they give us the powers to be the strongest guardians. A single bite of a Lupi may kill any creature of any species, including another Lupi; however not you. That is because you are an Alpha. Your blood is not the same as any other Lupi, therefore, a Lupi bite is not lethal to you unless it came from another alpha. Regardless, because of the Divine who originally cast the spell, should a Lupi bite one of their own kind, they become what is known as a Relecti. A mindless being that knows nothing but to kill. Their brains are scrambled far beyond any ability to comprehend, to have any remorse, any human emotion, and they become the most violent murderers. They lose all sense of their human-self, unable to shift back from their wolf form, but rather evolve into a creature far more deadly. A creature that's appearance matches the darkness of sin they committed when biting one of their own."

"So that wolf... the one who bit Lowell..." my question trails off.

"Yes, he will become a Relecti," Verena states with ease.

"Why would he do that?"

"This pack, these Lupi," her voice tenses as the word strains out of her mouth. "They are willing to do anything for their cause. In unum modicum: et regnabit ruber."

"My Latin is a bit rusty," I tease, attempting to translate what she said in my mind. That one semester I took Latin in high school is failing to help now. "To me, that was, 'The duck was dressed in a pig onesie.'"

"Close," she laughs. "But it's actually, 'With one bite, red shall reign."

"Very poetic," my eyebrows rise as sarcasm follows with my words.

"They appear to think so. Regardless, they are bloodthirsty, and when it comes to following orders, there is no length they wouldn't go to."

As we finally reach the camp after another few hours of walking, they immediately rush Caesar and Lowell to see the healer they mentioned from before. Pacing back and forth outside of the cabin they took Caesar into, my head hangs down and my eyes watch each step my feet take.

The mental image I had of the camp throughout the journey is squandered by the sights of what can only be described as a wolf town. Where I imagined tents and caves for sleeping, holes and dirt patches for bathrooms, are rather cabins covering most of the grounds. Wooden structures standing firm, most marked as sleeping quarters or a dining room, as they surround a large clearing that has racks of weapons. Both humans and wolves occupy the training grounds. From people shooting at an archery range, others sparring with swords, axes, staffs. The ample sound of wolves growling as they combat one another, shuffling through the grounds as they train.

While there are no restaurants or malls of such, there's a sense of a pleasing relief at the thought of me not having to go hunting to eat squirrels and sleep with weaved sticks and leaves for blankets.

Looking back into the cabin, I edge close enough to the door, open barely wide enough where I can peak through. My gaze glides across the room, human figures shambling throughout the room, orders being demanded and calling for things that sound as if they belong in a witches spellbook. Then I see him. His body spread over a tabletop as people surround him, stitching him up in one place and cutting into him in another.

There's a tight wrench in my heart as I back away from the cabin. I can't be here. I can't see him like this.

Twisting my head away from seeing inside, my body follows, turning away from the cabin. I can't be here right now. A heaviness grows within my chest as I walk away from the building, from him. Following a random trail along the camp, I traipse aimlessly before entering a treelines deeper into the forest hoping for a very welcomed distraction from all that is happening.

Through my exploring and wandering around, I stumble upon a place that could make the gods cry, tearing my breath away. In front of me lies a lake, one so clear it reflects the oranges and pinks of the visible sky above. A mirror for the trees and shadows that hang above. Water so still, it holds the whispers and wishes of all the creatures who find peace in this forest, from the elegant birds serenading above, to the fragile deer who graze. Winds saunter over the grass and past the trees, enough to brush my hair behind me, swaying with the fallen leaves. Fireflies fluttering between the flowers, glimmering the variations of color against their star-like shine. A land so tranquil, so pure. An enchanting force that makes me feel like I belong. Like I'm home.

"Serelia," a thick voice breathes from behind. A voice who's owner I've been waiting to hear since the moment I followed Caesar into this forest. A voice my mother knew so long ago, and the voice who years ago I never would have imagined to ever know.

Turning, I finally come face to face with the man who holds that same forest within his eyes as my own. The man who changed my life before he could even enter it. The man who is responsible for the Lupi in my blood.

"Hi, Dad."

Chapter 15

"You look like her." After all of the years imagining what I would want to say to my father, what he would say to me, all those moments of dreaming could have never prepared me for now. Observing every detail of him, studying his face, I try to find any link, any connection, between us. Though he holds the same green embers in his eyes, I've never expected to know him as more than a blurred face within my mind. Even to think of him as a name, but never an actual person, it made it easier to hate him. To not care for him. Yet here he is now in front of me.

Words escape and any possible response I could say is lost in my chest. 'Hey Dad, I know you abandoned me for almost eighteen years, but hey, since I'm a werewolf now, I guess it's time for a family reunion. Should I even mention all of those years that you missed, or should I get straight into saving your pack?' Probably not the best introduction.

The two of us stand frozen between the charms of pine greens and stillwater blues, rosewood red and a burning sun orange. Ancient trees casting shadows that shapeshift along the lush grass and dirt. Tears of sunlight kissing the ground and flowers sheltering themselves in the green below. My own personal slice of heaven, but a moment in hell.

"Funny, she used to say the same to me about you. Though, I could never see the resemblance before." Through the sarcasm that tries to emit with each word, a soft whimper follows behind. Damn it. Shaking my head, I force myself back towards the water. Picking up a small stone beside my foot, I skip it across the crystal lake.

One... two... three... I count the number of skips the smoothed rocked takes as ripples form in its trail. After a few more jumps, the weight of the stone allows it to be swallowed by the water below.

"I did what I had to. For your protection, for your mother's. There was no other choice to make," his voice remains steady as his words draw out.

I attempt to wait, knowing that anything I say in these next moments won't be what I truly want to say. My heart and my brain working against one another, being out of control of either. But eventually, like the stone that is now descended beneath the water, I sink.

"There's always another choice," my emotions consume me and any willpower is being pulled down with each second. The heaviness of my mind is drowning. "There is always another choice," I repeat, my voice more forceful now. "You didn't have the courage to look for one."

"If I had stayed, both of your lives would have been in danger."

"Look around," my arm rises up, gesturing to the forest around. "I am in danger right now. This great plan you forced on everyone has failed. I'm being hunted and had to leave behind everything I've ever known. But I made that choice. I made the choice to come here and help you. If you had ever wanted to stay, and wanted to truly protect us, you would have done it."

"I never wanted this for you, Serelia. I tried my best and if I had any other options..." His voice remains monotone, never once faltering as he remains in his place. "I never wanted you to be involved in this life. That's why I delayed your transformations, that's why I left. This isn't what I wanted for you or your mother."

"I saw you with her. You didn't seem to try so hard to keep her out of this life all those years ago. She would have never known about it if it weren't for you."

Aryce remains silent for a moment, only staring at me as I wait. "Your dreams... an ability so few ever have." He changes the subject. Well, there appears to be one connection between us. "I didn't know it was something you had gained until Caesar mentioned his visits with you. The last person I've known who had the sight was years ago, but before then, it had been decades. Perhaps that's why the incantation wore off before its normal time. It's not surprising, especially because of your mother. She has a rare gift so many Maleo's never possess—to believe in the unbelievable. She was special, and when I learned about her, I had to know her. To figure out why her. Instead, I fell in love..." He pauses once again, a quick gulp as his eyes break from my direction before bouncing back up as quickly. "I never wanted any harm to her. We had discussed leaving, going off somewhere far. She leaves Lupa Valley and I leave the pack, but those were plans from long ago."

"I'm guessing that those plans were changed because of you, weren't they?" I pick up another stone, skipping it across the waters and breaking its stillness once again.

"A few days before our departure, your mother had nearly been killed in an attack by a Lupi who refused to let me leave. I was going to lose her, one way or another, I made the choice that saved both of you."

"Well, it looks like that may happen anyway. Again, great plan."

"That isn't fair, Serelia. Please, know that," he steps closer, his arm reaching out for mine. His sentence breaks as I pull my arm away as he makes contact, taking another step away. A soft breath hushes from his lips. "Know that I tried, and that every day I have thought about you and this chance we have now."

"No!" All the anger and hurt I've been holding within bursts out without warning, exploding from my chest before I can think about what I'm saying. "Do you know what isn't fair? It's not fair that for every father's day, every birthday, every single moment I wished I had a dad, there was no one. It's not fair that I cried constantly because my father, a person that most kids need in their life, didn't want to be there for mine. I used to tell everyone you were dead. That seemed to be easier to cope with than the truth that you chose to leave us. For my whole life, I've lived with the belief that you left because you didn't love us, love me." I choke back a sob, my heart pounding in my chest. I can't find the words I want to say, yet words are all that seem to spill. "It isn't fair that after mom's accident, I had no one. That I had to learn to survive by myself, and now you literally want to throw me to the wolves. I've already lost you. I've lost mom. I've lost myself. And still I am here. But don't you dare to try to fight me about what is and isn't fair because trust me, I'll win." My final words batter out with venom, every ounce of pain he's put me through lacing with each sentence to ensure he knows what he's done to me.

There's a moment of guilt in his eyes, a brief pause where you can truly see the look of hurt on his face. His eyes take a fleeting glance down, clouded with the same misery I saw in my mother when I saw her last. But just as a moment only lasts for so long, his whole demeanor shifts from a gutted father to a soldier. "I know this is difficult for you. Regardless, your training must begin soon. There are many who are counting on you, Serelia. Despite how you feel about me, I need you to fight, to learn who you truly are here."

"I'm not a soldier. Two of your wolves got hurt trying to protect me," just as my father, all my emotion has abandoned me, rendering me numb. "How am I supposed to live with myself if one of them dies? If any one of your wolves dies for me because you all see me as some sort of leader. I'm barely able to grasp the fact that you all, that everything I thought were simply fairy tales, are real. Let alone accept that I am one. I'm not a leader. I never will be. The question is, how many of your people are you willing to sacrifice this war? The pack, my mother... me."

"Where your story began is not what defines you, Serelia. Your blood, what you choose in your life, that's what makes you who you are. Being raised as a Maleo does not make you any less of a Lupi. You might not believe you are a leader, and right now I won't be able to convince you otherwise, but here you will learn balance. You will experience what it means to be a Lupi and then you shall see that you are more than you think you are. As for sacrifice," he pauses as a breath hitches in his throat. "I would sacrifice myself before I ever let anything happen to you, Serelia."

My jaw clenches as he waits in silence. Seventeen years of abandonment and the pain that came with it heats within me hotter than any fire. I attempt to bite my lip to refrain myself from saying anything else, but unlike Aryce, I'm not as skilled at holding back my emotion. "If it comes down to it, save yourself." My voice is dry and the words can barely flow through without breaking with how much darkness fills them. "You already sacrificed me the day you decided to leave me. If you chose not to care about me then, I don't expect you to now."

Finally finding enough strength, I walk away. Don't look back. Isn't that what you're supposed to do? When you set off a bomb, simply move on without thinking twice, without ever looking back. That's what I am, a ticking bomb. One that just exploded, leaving nothing but pandemonium and havoc in my wake. Yet I am the one still standing, barely.

Making my way back to the center for camp, I hunt to find Caesar or at least any news on him. Finding my way back onto the training grounds, I scan the area to see plenty of Lupi scrambling at the different stations. A mix of limbs swinging back and forth, sharpened blades being gripped and wielded, skin glittering with sweat. Vitality and hunger pouring off each one of them.

I wonder what would happen if Maleos ever learned the truth of this world. Their world. My world, as it seems. To them, magic is something people see in a paid show, yet they always have more fun trying to unveil how each trick was pulled off. But here, there is no veil.

Verena called the Lupi warriors— protectors. What if there is something larger that they are protecting the human world from? Something more than this being they destined me to fight. What if there is something out there that's worse?

I know of one thing— the day my mother was dragged away nearly three years ago. My eyes glance down to the ring sitting upon my finger. My only connection to her while I'm here.

Pulling my attention back onto the Lupi training, I begin to notice those tattoo markings that I saw on Caesar from before. This time I'm able to see the mark so much clearer. How the black ink is painted on their skin, most of them on different parts of their bodies. But always the same mark. Arched and twisted lines trace along their skin, curving along to form a shape similar to an eye.

Spotting Verena coming out from one of the structures, I saunter my way to her anticipating any news on Caesar. As I reach about halfway to her, an unease begins to sway within me as I notice the serious look etched on her face.

Serelia. A light whisper fills my head. A female's voice, so soft I almost don't hear it. Then it becomes the only sound I hear. Freezing in place, I examine my surroundings to make out where the voice is coming from. You may have the forest within your eyes, but you will never be a true Lupi, Serelia Lone.

There.

As her final words echo inside of my mind, I spot a figure in a small clearing between the trees. A female figure crouches down, the shadows concealing her identity. Nothing recogniz-able to determine. The only thing I know is that she is watching me, and as she does, a hanging sense of trepidation weighs over me.

Though I'm unable to see her eyes, we stare at one another, glaring until one of us backs down from a silent fight. Not attacks, no movement— nothing. Our time will come. Then, just like that, without ever seeing her face, I know exactly who this is. Get your affairs in order. Soon enough, your story shall end with your blood spilling amongst your pack.

A compulsion itches me to fight, to push forward and con-front her here and now; however, it is without a doubt she would kill me before I could ever even reach ten feet of her. She knows this and it fuels her heart, one that radiates with pure darkness, silently taunting me to give into my urges and fight a battle I know I will lose. Go. You have to go. My impulse emits a strength drawing me forward. Just one step...

Chapter 16

"Hey, are you okay?" Verena's voice halts the compulsion that nearly consumed me. She closes the far gap between us until she's now only a few feet from me.

"Did you hear her?" I ask, but glimpsing back to where I had seen the figure, she's vanished. From all that I have seen, it's not just me who should be able to hear the whispers, yet no one seems to have noticed that she was here. Why was it only me?

"Her who?" Verena flicks her eyes over to the treeline where I'm still inspecting, looking for any indication where she went. "Serelia?"

"Her. I think it was her," I say before Verena's eyes fill with understanding. "I think-" I hesitate, "I'm sure of it."

"How is it that she could have gotten past the patrol? Someone would have alerted us of any Crimson Children nearby," her eyes land back onto mine and I'm sure she can sense the panic within them. "I'll send out some of the others to go check to make sure everything is okay. That's where you saw her?" Her head tips up toward the treeline uphill and I nod in response.

She calls out a few of the Lupi in the training area, two of them who had traveled back to the camp with us, Balor and Lycus. They assure me that we're safe, that I'm safe, and that everything will be okay. Though, I somehow have a hard time believing that.

"How is everything?" I turn back to Verena after Balor and Lycus leave us. "Where's Caesar?"

"He's...recovering. Very slowly recovering. He's been in and out of consciousness for a while, but they're hopefully for a full recovery."

"And Lowell?"

"His condition hasn't improved as much. They are saying his wounds are deep and are worried if the bite got too far into his bloodstream. We're worried there's not much that can be done for him, at this point only time will tell."

"Can I see him?" My words spill out soft as I think about both Caesar and Lowell.

Making our way to the recovery complex, my gaze immediately falls to Caesar lying on one of the beds. His skin drenched in sweat, drips beading along his forehead. His eyes remain closed, but his breathing appears more steady than before. A thin sheet rests at his feet, black sweatpants covering his legs while his abdomen is bare. Cuts and bruises line along his chest, his arms, his neck. Healing wounds, but still very visible.

I can't ignore the wrenching that pulls in my heart as the sun's light shines onto Caesar's wounds—a spotlight that highlights my doing. What has happened because of me, because he came to me for help, and that is exactly what I failed to do.

Sitting at the foot of the bed beside him, a faint groan emits past his lips.

"Caesar," Verena's pained voice hints with relief as Caesar's eyes flutter open. Placing her hand upon his forehead, she says. "Your fever's breaking. Also gross, why are you so sweaty?" She rubs her palm against the bed sheet, damping the thin fabric.

"Don't tell me you're freaked out by a bit of sweat, Pawlus," he responds with a sluggish rasp. "We've all had our fair share on these beds, you know how it is." His eyes draw down towards me, his gaze meeting mine. "I'm a survivor, Doll. No need to worry about a couple of scratches."

A thin smile rises on my lips, but deep down there's a solace in seeing him talk with normality. Before I can respond, Balor and Lycus enter the room. They walk with a tense, soldier-like stature, both boys standing tall with a face of no emotion, still as soon as they come in, I know something is wrong.

"Alpha, you should see this. Your father is already on sight waiting for us to meet him."

There's a brief dismay as they look at me, but there is no way I will know how to handle a situation like this. I barely found out I'm supposed to be an alpha, but I'm still trying to figure out what that even means.

"I'll go," Verena interferes. "Take me to Aryce," the boys lead her out while discreetly talking to her on their way out.

"What was that about?" He readjusts himself on the bed to where he's now sitting up, his back leaning against the wall to hold him steady.

"I saw her, Caesar. She was here, in the camp."

"That's impossible," he states, my words having absolutely no effect on him. "There are guards to ensure no outsiders enter the camp, not within a mile radius of us. Also adding onto the fact that while we know she's out there, someone has yet to have seen her."

"I know what I saw," I counter, my fingers playing with the blanket. "She was here."

"Alright," he shifts his body again, swinging his feet off of the other side from where I sit and sitting next to me. His shoulder presses against mine, a damp warmth spreading on top of my skin rests besides me. While his body faces the wall behind me, I can feel his burning stare presses along my being. "Was there anything you noticed about her? Any recognition or anything you can describe?"

"She was too far away for me to see her. I only heard her voice, but even then it was too quiet to notice anything aside from the fact that it felt cold.""Cold?"

"I can't explain it. I heard her voice the same way I used to hear yours, the wolves. She called out to me in my mind. But she caused something within me that made me want to fight, even knowing what could happen. I didn't have any control. And the only way I can describe it is that it felt cold." I pause, remembering how it wasn't until Verena came that snapped me out of pursuing her. "But that doesn't change the fact that I know it was her."

"Hey," his hand hesitates towards me before shifting direction and landing on the bed. "I believe you," his demeanor softens. "We'll figure this out. I promise you that."

Tipping my head back up, my sight catches on his eyes. The hazel tone of his eyes casting a warming glow, an autumn sun with the infusion of his own spring forest resting in his stare. Our eyes linger on one another as we sit here in silence. His face is not far from mine and I can feel the heat of his breath brushing down at me. A slow but heavy breath matching my own, emitting his smell that I've come to easily recognize, cinnamon and pine. There's a fluttering in the pit of my stomach, a similar vibration beating in my heart. Nerves spreading of what he will finally say, finally do.

Without either of us saying a word, I can still hear everything Caesar has to say. A look of understanding, of comfort.

"We should go catch up with the others," he whispers, breaking our world of silence.

Without saying anything, my head nods and I push myself up from the bed as Caesar does the same. As we leave the cabin, I follow Caesar as he walks towards the dining area outside, Lupi scattered amongst the tables.

"I have a question for you," I speak up as we walk, me trying to keep up with him as his strides move much larger than mine. "How did you know the wolf that attacked us? You said his name before everything happened."

"Alba Cicatrix," his head tilts down as his stature is much taller than mine. "I had never met him until today, but I've heard the legends. His scar, the one across his eye. According to what's been told in the stories, there was an inner war between his pack. Their alpha from the time had gone corrupt, fighting a war that would have led to the deaths of many, including their own. As this war progressed, other alpha's began to stop them. Aryce, loyal to his alpha, ended up scratched by one of them, losing his eye in the process. Lupi heal quickly, but any wound procured by an alpha remains forever."

"What happened to their alpha?"

"That's a question for another day," he states. "You've already taken in so much. Let it rest for a minute so you don't worry about what is not yet important." Though, the wrenching in my stomach only tightens as I wonder what this could mean for this new war.

"Well if it isn't the infamous sleeping beauty making his return to society," one of the Lupi calls out as we near the tables where he sits by himself, a tray of food resting in front of him on the wooden foundation. Caiden, one of the Lupi who helped carry Caesar back to camp— one of Caesar's closest friends according to Verena. From what she had described, they've been in a competition ever since Caesar and her joined the camp, but that competition is also what has brought them so close together.

"Only a couple of flesh wounds," Caesar remarks back to him.

"Perhaps if you hadn't been so slow to attack, the coward of a Lupi would have never been able to take the advantage," Caiden continues, but a teasing grin rests on his face as he speaks. His eyes flash into a cider brown as we move to sit. "And this must be our new reigning alpha," he says, though I don't respond as my eyes dance across the camp before freezing. "A quiet one, isn't she?" Though, I down out his words as I stare at the figure off in the distance, the faint mutters of the two continuing their conversion at the table.

Aryce. I watch him as he strolls back into the camp along with others besides him— returning from the treeline where I had seen the earlier figure. Verena separates from their group, her now coming to the table we sit at and I sense her at the seats across from me, but my eyes keep on him.

He stops along the training area with another, both grabbing daggers from one of the nearby racks before moving across from one another in a defensive stance. I watch as they engage in quick, swift motions against each other, becoming entranced as their motions go through so clean and dignified. There's not a single moment of hesitation as they both swipe their silver blades, dodging the other. The metal clinging as the air around fills with a harsh and thundering cling. Both men dance as if they had rehearsed each motion a thousand times before, moving together as if one were looking in a mirror. Ease in each step and swing, an aggressive intensity with each movement forward— an enthralling performance.

"Hey," a nudge pushes against my arm. Shaking out of my reverie, I drift my attention back to the table, a collection of eyes all on me.

"I'm sorry, what were you saying?" I ask, though there was not a single clue in my mind about what their conversation is about.

An amusing snort sounds from Caiden as Verena says, "About tonight." Though, there must be a clear confusion written across my face as I sit silent. "We're throwing the celebration tonight," she speaks slowly to see if I can comprehend what she's saying, but nothing registers.

"What are we celebrating?"

"You," Caesar's words beat from beside me. My eyebrows raise, furrowing together as I look for further clarification as to what they're talking about.

A quick sigh draws from Verena. "You are the reigning alpha making your return. There is a tradition that when a new alpha comes to rule, we celebrate," her voice perks up with a light enthusiasm. "It's one of the largest of our kind in fact, many don't ever get to experience it as the changing of alpha's is not so common."

"The long lost alpha coming to her reign," Caiden snickers.

"I'm not the alpha yet," I inform. "I haven't done anything yet. Hell, I've barely even been here a day."

"By blood," Caesar says, "you have been here the entire time. You just hadn't known it yet. But for a long time, we have been awaiting your arrival."

"Besides," Verena says, her words still coming out excitedly as we discuss the event. "It's the perfect introduction for you into this life, to where you come from. Plus, we hardly ever get any nights off for something like this."

"Can I ask something?" I switch from the current conversation. "Do you ever visit the Maleo world? I mean, you all can't simply stay here in the forest for your entire lives, can you?"

"It's not uncommon, but also pretty frowned upon by the elders here," Verena answers. "Some Lupi, though, they visit a lot. A few even have human relations there, another life separate from this one."

"Verena of course would know about the human relations with Maleo life," Caiden teases. "She's gone to the Maleo society for her share of fun, haven't you?" He glances at her with a taunting expression.

"Haven't we all," Verena argues back. "Besides, the way you Maleo all live, it's truly something else. Though, despite how breathtaking it may be, especially with how unpredictable it is, the Virunis life is everything to me. I wouldn't trade the forest or our lives for anything else. Caesar on the other hand here, I almost believe he wants to live in the Maleo world at times." Her thumb flicks across to her brother who tilts his head down at the table. A light flush draining in his cheeks as he gets called out.

"I'm not sure," I respond. "I don't know where I fit in. This world, the Maleo world. If I fit into either of them. I can barely understand who I am at times, let alone where I stand."

"One of the most difficult challenges to face is not deciding who you want to become, but rather allowing yourself to be who you are. But once you find that, you'll grow stronger than you are now," Caesar says, his words soft enough that I can barely hear them fully. "For us, we have always known who we are, you are barely learning. Give it time."

Verena interrupts, finishing Caesar's thoughts. "Runes, incantations, potions, and species are enough of what you're going to have to learn in this world, and that's something we'll help you with, but your identity is something you'll get to discover for yourself."

Before I have any chance to say anything further, Aryce approaches our table. My head shifts past Verena's head across the table, averting my sight anywhere from my father.

He stands close by me, a grim energy and a sense of desolation hinting off of him. There's a deep release of breath before he speaks.

"Lowell didn't make it," Caesar cuts in before Aryce has the chance to utter a word. His voice has gone flat as he asks, all emotion that was there prior now gone.

I don't see Aryce, but from the sudden intensity I feel from Caesar besides me and the brief shift from Verena, I know that Aryce confirmed what everyone has been dreading.

"The Crimson Children are going to answer for all of the death they have brought to our pack," Verena's teeth grit against each other as she speaks.

"That will be for another day," Aryce declares. "Soon they will face the consequences of their actions. For now, we must prepare Serelia to lead. Caesar, if you are healed completely tomorrow, I will need you to begin her training immediately. Verena, she shall stay with you in your cabin," his voice speaks with authority.

"We'll start at breaking light," Caesar directs to me. "We don't have much time otherwise."

"It's nearly dusk," Verena chimes in. "If you will start that early on, you both need to ensure you're rested and healed fully. Serelia," my gaze falls back down onto her. "Whenever you are ready, we'll head over to my cabin." Listlessly nodding in response, I remain silent, processing all that has happened today alone.

No matter how much of this new life I acknowledge, I barely have enough time to comprehend it before another drastic event happens and decides to yank me down once more, proving to me this is a life I could have never imagined.

"Get ready, Alpha," Caesar says. "Tomorrow will be the first day of your new life."

Chapter 17

I t's only been a couple of days since I found Caesar in my bedroom back home and learned the truth about who I am, what I am. Only a couple of days since I was a normal girl who thought nothing in this lifetime could surprise me anymore. A couple of days ago, I thought I was human. It turns out that a lot more can change in only a couple of days than anyone truly gives credit for.

After we received the news about Lowell, no one was really in the mood to celebrate my return home that night, instead deciding to wait until after his funeral. Since that day, Caesar and I have mostly been training for the majority of hours in our days. According to him, we're seventeen years behind, which essentially means that aside from eating and sleeping, perhaps an occasional shower, all I'm really doing is training.

Sitting inside of Verena's cabin, I scope out what constitutes a living room, though there isn't much life to be led inside of these walls. The cabin is nothing grand, but rather a mid-sized, cherry-wooden structure. There are only a few, but large windows that line against the walls allow the sunlight to creep in through. Vines and moss cover the window edges, tracing along the glass panes with flowers and trees bordering around, making the outside look as if this was straight out of a fairy tale.

Inside, there's a vast bookcase that covers nearly an entire wall in the living room. Most of the books are covered in light specks of dust, some of them in English, but the majority in Latin or some other foreign language. There's a red sofa in the center of the room, the one I currently sit on, that has a few patterned cushions on top, but the sofa itself still feels unbroken. As if it's hardly ever been worn out. Across from me lies a stone fireplace, no sense of ash splaying around and no logs that have any trace of ever being burned stacked inside.

The only sign of evident life in this room is the training gear scattered around, most notably on the dining table in front of me are her twin axes. It's rare that she's ever without them. Leaning forward to the table, I reach my hand out and graze my fingertips along the navy blue handles on the axes, feeling the textured markings that swirl to form different runic designs on both.

"It means balance," Verena pipes up behind me, her footsteps beating against the wooden floor as she shuffles around the couch. She reaches down to the table and gently picks up one of her axes, brushing her thumb over one of the glyphs that resembles a letter 'A' with two circles on either side. She slides her finger down to wording slanted across the handle, whispering, "Quamdiu ego sum fortis, ego sum, et humana. For as long as I am a warrior, I am also human."

"What does it mean?" My eyes bounce backward from her face to the axe in her hand, watching as she studies the symbols along the blade and handle.

"One of the biggest struggles a Lupi shall face is choosing which side they choose to fight for, the light or the dark. For me, in order for me to survive, I remember that I can be both. Both strong and weak, powerful and gentle, and most importantly, to be able to perceive both the beauties and horrors of life," she pauses. "We lose so much, but I remind myself that there is also so much that is magical, so much that is meaningful in what we do."

"All of this, everything that's happened, it's so much more than I could have ever expected."

"You had expectations when it comes to being a Lupi and moving to a forest filled with magic and wars?" She says with a lace of sarcasm, a soft smile reaching both her lips and eyes.

"Well one thing's for sure, I underestimated how much I would miss having the internet, of any sorts," I chuckle.

"We may live in two separate worlds, but we do have our commonalities. Though, I know you'll find your place here. I have the feeling that you're exactly where you're meant to be," she moves to sit in the empty space on the couch next to me.

"There is still one thing I have wondered about," I smile, twisting my body so I can better face her. Also managing to change the topic that she tried to sneak in there at the end.

"What's that?" She responds, not phased by my shifting the subject.

"Okay, so in every story I've ever heard about werewolves, prior to coming here at least, after a transformation, they lose their clothes. Is that true?"

It takes a few seconds of Verena laughing before regaining her composure to speak. "Fairy tales in your Maleo sense are nearly similar to our more historical aspects. There was a time when that was true, Lupi would lose their clothes in the process of transforming, but that wasn't exactly ideal for when we shift back into humans," she giggles as she talks. "Fatals gave us an enchantment to avoid that happening many years back, sparing many future awkward transformations between us. Thankfully so, as well, or else I would have lost many endearing outfits."

She laughs a little before speaking up, already knowing where I was heading with my question. "It wasn't always where we got to keep our clothes. Before, those parts of the stories were true, but obviously it wasn't always ideal for us when we turn human again, so the Fatals put an enchantment so we can avoid that happening. Spare a lot of awkward moments between us, which I can just say is a blessing because if not I would have lost a lot of cute outfits." We both start laughing at this and just keep talking for a bit about other Virunis creatures and the forest.

We spend a while chatting and laughing, Verena answering many more of my questions about the Lupi world as she asked me of my life before here. We both decided to get some sleep as it was almost the break of light. Another full day of training ahead of me.

Walking into my room, one which I've become more familiar with in these last couple of days, I go to one of the dressers to take out some pajama clothing to wear. Once changing into some comfier sweatpants and a matching sports bra, I roam around the room, still taking it in.

With a boho-type style to it, the room is colored a delicate, vanilla-yellow shade with paintings lining against the walls. The largest one is an abstract oil painting, hues of greens and browns to create the making of a forest that hangs above my bed. The sheets are covered with an intricate and colorful paisley pattern on top. Two lamps with golden, metal rods stand against the corners of one of the walls, a cedar-wooden wardrobe in between with a standing mirror next to it.

At the desk near my bedside sits a dusted acoustic guitar. My instincts call out to me and draw me to reach out for it, picking it up from its lazy sitting position against the wall. Sitting on top of the wooden chair in front of the desk, my hands graze against the strings, by memory recognizing some of the chords my mom had taught me to place once upon a time.

When she bought me my first guitar I refused to set it down until I managed to perfect a new song, putting on a small concert for my mother when I finally managed to strum each chord flawlessly. She used to teach me how to write poetry, those which later turned into lyrics. For grandma, she was more into the visual arts, paintings done at her hands hung in each of the rooms at her house.

There is a distant sense of familiarity to my old room here with the art and alternative styles. A nostalgia slaps me across the face thinking back to my life before the wolves, a deep pain pulling at my heart at the thoughts of grandma and my mom.

My lips press together as I put the guitar back to its place against the wall. Turning off the remaining lights, I lie down in the bed despite the lack of being tired, simply staring at the ceiling as the shadows from the moon's light dance across the canvas above. Soon, my eyes hesitate as they close, my body drifting off to sleep. As soon as I do, the nightmares begin.

My eyes snap open, beating against my eyelids as I sit up. Something's off. The immediate sense overwhelms me as I gather my surroundings. Something is different from when I fell asleep. A white light blurring my vision of everything around, though, as my sight begins to clear, there's a quick realization that I am no longer in Verena's cabin.

I don't even think I'm in the forest anymore.

Looking down, a white gown drapes over my body as I sit on top of clean, fresh white sheets of my bed. Aside from the bed that I sit on, the confined, shining room is primarily empty besides a steel desk to my left. What the hell? There's something familiar about this place. I've been here before, but all memories of such are completely lost to me.

The white walls of the room give the illusion of a strong sun blazing inside, but in reality, the only window along these walls sits high up, only the pale blue sky painted through. The other is one that shows through the single door in front of me, a small gap to reveal more white walls outside.

Lifting myself off of the bed, I walk over to the door to peek through the small pane of glass, a long hallway on the other side. Nothing distinct enough to recognize where I am.

A woman appears on the other side of the door, her ginger hair in a tight bun showing through the dainty window as she opens the door. Stepping back, I stare as she enters the room. A nurse's gown covering her petite body. She lets off a feeble smile as she spots me, turning back into the hallway to drag in a tall cart that carries stainless-steel instruments. On top sits a stack of needles, a plastic cup filled with ten different colored pills, and other tools scattered about.

"You're awake," she says with a feathery voice. Her smile never breaks, almost eerily, as she moves about the room.

"Where am I?" I mutter to her, though my words come out hoarse.

"How are you feeling today, Miss Lone?" The woman asks, not acknowledging my question.

"Where am I?" I repeat, a bit louder now though my vocal chords strain as I do.

"This is- Is everything okay, dear? Did the nurse come by earlier to give you your medications this morning?"

Becoming more irritated as she avoids answering my question, I ask again after swallowing a gulp that harshly swells down my throat. "I have no idea what you're talking about, lady. Where is Verena? Where's Caesar?"

"Miss. Lone, have you been attending your therapy sessions?"

"Therapy? What? What are you talking about?" I become more frantic with her vague responses, my body beginning to tremble as fear tangles inside of me. "Who are you? Where am I?" I near the woman as she fumbles with some of the objects on the tray, my presence closer and the spurting of my questions causing her to tense up and spin in my direction.

"Miss. Lone, is everything alright with you, dear? I highly recommend attending your sessions, they are mandatory as you know," she mumbles something beneath her breath, her words spoken so softly they are completely indistinguishable. "Your mother has been going and she seems to be feeling better herself."

"My mother?" Recognition hits me like a sucker punch as I suddenly realize where I am. How? There's no way. It's impossible. Fear goes from being tangled inside of my heart to now bursting out out my chest and exploding through the rest of me. "I am going to ask you one more time," my voice raises to where I am now yelling in this woman's face. I don't care though. "Where am I?"

The lady heaves a heavy sigh while looking out into the hallway before back at me. "Miss. Lone, this is Home for Angels. You're safe here. Please, take this medication," she picks up the small cup from the tray and pushes it in my direction. "You need to calm down before I call for security."

My breaking quickens before turning into a sharp pant. This can't be happening. There's no way. My hands grab at my scalp, holding onto chunks of my hair as my head drops down, my mind spinning out of control. Tears well in my eyes. My biggest fear is being lived out in front of me. But how is it real?

You're dreaming. You have to be. You have to be dreaming.

Grabbing a piece of my arm, I pinch together my skin between my nails and squeeze as hard as my strength permits.

"Wake up," I hiss as I continue to pinch myself in different spots along my arm. Nothing works. "Wake up!" The pain worsens, not just on my arm, but my mind as it believes more and more that this is truly happening.

"Miss. Lone," the nurse pries my fingers away from my arm. "Please, settle down now. Security!" She shouts out the door and I try to yank myself free from her grasp. Tears now spilling, lingering as they fall down my face. Shaking my head, whatever I can to wake myself up.

The woman's robotic smile is now twisted into a frown as she watches me breakdown in front of her. "Security!" She shouts again before turning back to me. "Miss. Lone, I need you to compose yourself. Calm down. You must take your medication."

She attempts to shove the pill cup at me once again, but I slap the plastic out of her hands. All of the small capsules plummeting to the ground. Because of her being much smaller in size than me, with ease, I'm able to push her off of me and send her onto the ground with the dispersed pills.

Get out. You need to get out. Go back to the forest. Go home. Anywhere. Just get out of here.

Darting down the corridor, passing by the rooms holding other people who have been locked in these cells. A jail within these walls and within their own minds. Glancing back behind me, the nurse stays back in the distance, a cell phone pressed against her ear causing me to pick up my pace as I frantically search for an exit.

As I reach a much too familiar hallway, I ensure there's no one chasing from behind before I slow down. 35C... The doors and their plastered signs skim by as I continue hurrying through the hall. 40D... I hurtle past a few more, nearing my destination. Only stopping when I reach the room—her room.

If this is real and when I walk through this door, she will be there and hopefully can explain to me what is happening here.

Please don't be in there. This is my only chance to prove that this is all merely a terrible nightmare.

Stepping into the threshold, the inkling of hope I had plunges down as soon as I see her. "Mom," the word whispers in defeat as I spot her. More tears pool in my eyes before pouring down my face. She's unfazed by my presence, continuing to read the book resting in her hands. Alice Adventures in Wonderland. Her favorite story. One I heard a million times as a child every night when she put me to bed. Creeping closer to her, I face her back as her head remains leaning down to her book. "Mom," I repeat in a more onerous tone. The tip of my fingers extending to her shoulder, only to make contact with unearthly, cold skin.

As soon as my hand touches her, her head whips around to me. Only, it's not her. Not really at least.

A scream pierces from my throat, snatching my hand off from her and stumbling backwards. Her eyes are vacant. Instead of their normal, honey color, they are replaced with a white so bleak it matches everything else within this hospital. Her expression holds no sense of emotion, so withdrawn it barely even looks like her, but instead something of a monster. A low growl rumbles from her chest as she stands, trudging my way.

"Run," she says with a near demonic and strangled snarl. She continues to advance towards me until she's almost hovering right over me. "Run."

Picking myself up and sprinting out of the room, the echo of heavy footsteps follow close behind. The pounding of feet racing only a few steps in back of me, so burdensome, they sound like the harsh beat of a dream. I don't ever stop, too afraid to take a single glimpse back.

My feet want to give out, a searing struggle burning in my legs the more I run, but as I make out the Exit sign up ahead, I only push harder.

More footsteps come from behind, followed by claws scratching against the walls. A boiling breath huffing down my legs as I sense bladed teeth skimming along my bare skin.

I'm almost to the exit.

I can almost feel the light of freedom.

But I never make it there. A sharp and smoldering pain sinks into my legs, jerking me back and I fall forward, only stopping myself from landing on my face. "No!" I scream, but there is no one nearby to come save me. The burning spreads through my limbs, lurching me back despite my clawing on the tile ground to try and stop them. But in a matter of mere seconds, I am snatched into the darkness.

A penetrating scream escapes as my body jerks up. My eyes press shut, afraid of being further consumed by any darkness or anything that may be in front of me when I open them.

"Serelia," a female's voice says, a gentle hand grabbing hold onto my shoulder and I throw my hands in front of me in an attempt to fight off whatevers here with me. "Hey, it's me. Serelia, open your eyes. You're safe. You had a nightmare."

It takes a long second before I realize it's Verena's voice. With alarming caution, my eyes peek open only to reveal that I am still in my bedroom. I'm still in the forest. Though the panic within me doesn't drain. Trying to adjust to my surroundings, a deep inhale scorches as it streams down my chest, my adrenaline still in fight or flight.

"I'm okay," I reassure, Verena or myself though is what I'm unclear of. Regardless, I don't think either of us believe those words right now. "I'm going to go take a walk. I need to clear my head for a minute."

"Serelia-" Verena tries to comfort me and hold me down, though I don't give her the chance to continue. Rising out of my bed, I race out of the room before she can try and stop me.

Darting deeper into the forest, the memories of the nightmares still plaguing my mind. I don't take any notice of my surroundings until I collide into a heavy force, one that knocks me down the instant I make impact with it.

"Late night strolls, Doll?" Caesar's amused voice breaks me out of my trance. Picking my head up to look at him, his head hovering above me. Despite the entertainment absorbed along his face, I don't fail to notice the tinge of worry behind his eyes.

"I figured I'd get a head start on our training for today," I go to push my hands against the ground to pick myself up, but before I struggle to do so, Caesar's arm stretches down to me. Bringing my arm out in front of me, time slows as I reach up and connect my hand to his. His calloused skin sends a tingling through my palm and into my veins as I unequivocally accept his help. "I thought if I started early, maybe I'd be better off today, instead of your usual knocking my ass to the ground... again."

As we stand face-to-face, his hand is still interlaced with mine, his touch tender against my own. He exhales in a soft sigh. "Come with me. I want to show you something."

"What is it?"

"Do you trust me?" He takes a step back, curious if I will choose to follow him.

Though, we both know without hesitation what my answer is, which leads me to copying him and taking a step forward.

Trailing behind him as we hike through the forest, I'm unsure if I can find this place familiar as there is nothing identifiable of where we are. "Where are you going?" A scratch swells along my throat as I speak, still tense ever since waking up. The further we walk, the more my fatigued body begins to weigh down. Though, even if I was still at the cabin, I know sleep is the last thing I would possibly be doing right now.

"You'll see."

Chapter 18

As we walk in silence, the memories of my dream tease me. My head develops a dwindling fuzz in my efforts to concentrate on the forest around me, anything to distract myself enough. Though, nothing seems to be working as the only thoughts that occupy my mind are of my mother's face. Her voice.

"If this is about why I was outside, I'm telling you that I'm fine." Though, the lie emits with a hint of stuttering. I'm not even able to believe my own words as they utter through my mouth.

"Serelia," Caesar halts in his tracks. There's a slight tug in his grip as he turns to look back at me, a soft smirk pressing on his lips as his eyes peer along my face. There's a suggestion of levity in his eyes as he further purses his lips closed together, knowing he caught me in my weak attempt of a lie. His thumb fiddles over my own as he thinks of what to say. "You tend to forget I have the ability to hear what you're thinking," he confronts, though his voice is gentle as he speaks. "Besides," he spins back around and pulls on my hand for us to keep moving. "Even if that wasn't the case, you and I both know better than to believe that."

My feet drag deeper through the soil with the more trees we pass. The scent of wet grass and leaves fill my noise the further we trek uphill. Fireflies shine through thin blades of grass and overhead between the empty gaps between the trees. The moonlight breaks through where it can. It's luminescence showering faint teardrops of light, leaping over my skin. There's a faint song of crickets and the cracking of branches in the distance. The cool air sends my skin in shivers, a breeze that only strengthens the higher up we move.

It isn't until there is nowhere physically left for us to walk before Caesar finally stops. My lungs suck in a gasp as I take in the view ahead.

No longer surrounded by trees or dirt, we stand high up on a suspended cliff. A painted navy sky reveals a serene night, the radiance of the moon now clear and at eye-level. Its waning presence is like a giant eye starting down upon us, each creator visible as if looking through a telescope. The stars splatter about, some burning brighter and forming a series of shapes throughout the sky's canvas, a series of stories. My eyes follow along the patterns, silently naming the constellations as I make them out. Scorpius, Centaurus, Libra, Lupus...

Inching closer to the edge, I peer down to see only a silhouette of greens. Trees standing like noble giants far below, their sway with a hushed whistling as their limbs fork out in every direction. A faint glint of water can be seen running through a path below, separating the trees as the further along my eyes follow, the slow rapids bloom into a river that swims between the rocks and grit beside.

Taking a few steps back, attempting to gain a stable stance on the jagged rock, my eyes —where the world breaks in two.

"Tell me what you're thinking."

"Shouldn't you already know?" I keep my eyes looking ahead. Caesar's presence creeps closer behind me.

"Perhaps," his eyes pierce into my back and I can feel his hesitation to draw closer, so instead, he watches me from a slight distance. It would only take one or two steps backwards for my body to be pressed right against his. Even here, his protection for me never falters. Ready in case I were to slip. "I'd rather hear it coming from you."

"Honestly?" In his silence, I turn, so rather than seeing the world ahead, I'm looking at him. "I'm not sure anymore."

"It's not unsureness that stops you. You have the answers residing within you, but something is stopping you from admitting them. Not just to me now, but to yourself."

"I don't- I can't-" Words boil inside, struggling to find a voice that can speak them into existence. "I'm not sure if I can do this. Any of this."

Guilt burns alongside those unspoken words. Guilt about every moment I claimed my mother was crazy, dismissing her entirely from my life. The guilt of when I heard Caesar calling for me in the forest. Him lying on the ground, me unable to save him. That deepening wound of not knowing how I can possibly save everyone.

Caesar takes a step closer, my gaze only able to peer onto him. The wind dries the unfallen tears that brim.

"It wasn't your fault. Nothing has been your fault. None of what's happened now and before. Everyone, we all knew the battles that would be faced long before your arrival here. We are in a war, death is inevitable and-" My eyes shut as he speaks, that darkened thought of more people having to die is another nightmare I don't want to endure. A heated breath exhales from my nose, my head shakes as it droops low. Those unfallen tears begin to sting, forcing my eyelids together and never wanting to part. A gentle warmth presses against my chin. A light nudge lifting my head upwards, his gaze compelling my eyes open. As my eyelids peel from one another, the tears finally spill.

"It wasn't your fault," he repeats, emphasizing each word. His face inches from my own, pulling the breath from my lungs. "Serelia, you are not alone. Not in any battle or obstacle. Never again in this lifetime and any other one will you be alone."

"But-"

"No," he doesn't allow me to interrupt. "We are by your side in this battle. Your father, Verena, Meg, every Lupi in this pack will stand beside you in this war and long after."

"And you? Are you there besides me?"

A soft smile tugs at the corners of his lips. "Yes, I'm there. That's one thing you never have to doubt. That is how we're going to win against the Crimson Children, by trusting one another and moving forward, one step at a time"

His thumb lifts off of my chin only to push back a stray hair from my face. He tucks it behind my ear, but his touch lingers along my cheek. "Despite what you think or say, you are not some broken doll. You're strong. Too strong to let all that you are afraid of hold you back from who you are meant to be."

"And if I'm not sure yet? Of who I'm meant to be."

"You will." That's it. That is all he has to say, yet his confidence is steady with those two simple words. And the way he's looking at me now. His eyes, almost consuming me as undoubted hope sparks behind their hazel color.

Caesar grows silent with those final words, as do I. All there is in this moment is him, his hand pressed on the side of my face, our eyes locked together, and me.

A heat begins to rise beneath my skin. Goosebumps prickle across my arm, but not from the crisp bite of the night air. His hand is gentle against my skin, an unnerving flush stirs beneath his touch. An unsettling impulse beats beneath my chest with the quick thumps of my heart. The wolf is yelling at me with noiseless words, driving me from within. At least I hope it's the wolf. It has to be what's wanting to inch closer to him. Compelling me closer to him. To reach for his hand from atop my face, or to feel the beating of his chest. A thumping pressures against my eardrums, an unsteady rhythm playing. A soft melody that I can't tell belongs to my heart, or his.

My thoughts fade away the longer I look into Caesar's eyes. Only one left that I can hear. I don't want Caesar to look away. I don't ever want to look away.

There's a shift in his eyes, a realization that masks behind the shadows of his face and the dim gleam of the moon's light. His hand falls from my cheek and he breathes out a slight sigh that warms my skin for a brief moment. Shadows darken over his face and he straightens, his body towering over mine, but the heat of his body grows colder as he stiffens. It's as if a switch flicked within him, that intensity that lied behind his stare hardening into the stoic soldier he is.

Snapping out of the dazed trance he casted me into, I move closer to the cliff's edge and lower myself until I'm sitting. With nothing below my feet than a chilled air, I allow myself to become enchanted by the surroundings.

"Why did you bring me here?" Here being a world in between. A forest behind me, a forest in front of me, yet they are so different. The one behind holds danger and death. Its soil holds the blood of those who have fallen and the screams of those who have suffered. The one ahead holds mystery, holds the unknowing, and therefore I believe that it is full of magic and wonderment. Maybe flowers that shine like neon and some of the other creatures I was told of. Fairies and animals other than wolves. Then here we are, in the inbetween. "Of all places, why here?"

"That is another answer your mind should already possess."

My eyes jump around, counting the countless trees ahead. A lively laugh echoing from atop this extending rock. A true moment of cheerfulness despite how somber the night is. "Will I ever be able to ask you something that comes with a simple answer? Or should I be prepared to always have to decode everything you say?"

A quick laugh sounds from Caesar, but is one that just as quickly fades. "Wolves are fierce beings, wild and courageous creatures free from all that could hold us back. And we fight for our own until our last dying breath without fail. Though, as Lupi, one of our biggest faults is that we can never admit to the pain. You have your unsureness of this life, of being one of us, yet you hold this trait that so many bear. Though you sit here now, it wasn't so long ago that you would have jumped."

A memory skips in my brain. Finding my way into the forest, the wolf attacking yet never killing me. The moments before, wanting to find the edge of a world. Of jumping off of the edge of the world.

"You were there?" The words strain from my voice, a slight croak as the recollection strikes. How broken I was before discovering this world. How broken I still am even in this world. How long it's been since I lived in that world.

Another realization strikes and I open my mouth to speak again for an answer I'm not sure I want, but one that I need. "Were you the wolf that chased me? The one from that day?"

"Yes." The word sounds easy from Caesar. Bewilderment fills in both my eyes and heart as I snap my head to face him.

"What? Why? Why would you do that? Why would you attack me?" The questions spurt from my mouth. That single word of confirmation repeating in my head, unable to process that he was the one who chased me that day. Despite my panic, his expression is unwavering.

"It wasn't an attack," he collectively justifies, still unnerved as he speaks. "I was protecting you."

"Protecting me?" I attempt to move away from him, but his eyes hold me in place. I need to wait, to stay here and hear whatever else he has to say. "You attacked me. How is that supposed to be protection?" Has he been playing me this entire time? What reason would he have to do that to me? Then with everything we've been through after that. My mind can't unravel, spiraling as the questions only continue. "I don't understand, how is that protection? Protection from what?""From yourself," he says, growing silent again. The questions in my mind hush and I don't open my mouth to speak further. I need him to say more. "Your thoughts, everything you were thinking on that day," he pauses, his face finally faltering as I can see his eyes shift across. As if he's trying to think of the right words next. "In that moment, if you did reach some cliff... would anything have stopped you from truly jumping?"

Yes. I would have stopped.

Or at least that's what I want to believe. To be able to tell myself. But even the deepest conscious of my being knows that if those words came out of my mouth, they would be false. I know that at that moment, I would have jumped with no hesitation. Even now, I can imagine myself running on that day, reaching the end of the world and still creeping closer until there was nothing but air beneath me. Dying before I could even touch the ground.

That day processes in my mind, how things would have turned out differently if he wasn't there. How I wouldn't be here now if I kept running. Knowing that it was me who was the biggest danger in that moment, not the wolf inside of me, and not the monster I believed was lurking in the shadows. Well, not a monster that wanted to kill me. That was all me.

"And so you saved me." He's always saved me. Even from me.

As the thought crosses my mind, he shifts slightly from where he sits. There's a brush of his hand near mine and his heat further envelopes me. The scent of pine and cinnamon masking over the cool air of the forest. In a quick glimpse up to him, I see a soft smile pressed on his lips, though he doesn't say anything and only looks ahead now.

Did he hear me right now? My thoughts?

"Just..." I again move to be closer to Caesar, my arm further brushing against his. "Don't do it again. Don't scare me like that." The sentence plays off of my tongue with a lighthearted warning.

"No promises, Doll." There's an ease in his words, almost one of relief, as if he himself was worried about my reaction to the truth. Did he think I would no longer trust him if I knew? Is that why he wanted only till now to tell me?

"I thought I wasn't a doll. At least according to you?" I tease in a subtle attempt to show him that everything is okay. Showing me that everything is okay.

His smile grows slightly, a soft chuckle at my words. His head turns so he is again looking in my direction. "I said you weren't some broken doll. You will always be my doll."

With a growing smile, I bend my elbow and pull my arm slightly so that it hits him in his ribs.

The silence threatens to overcome the still winds. Another look of puzzlement crosses over Caesar. "Do you want this life?" He almost whispers the question, almost low enough that I didn't hear them. But I did.

"What do you mean?" I know exactly what he means, but still a part of me hopes that I'm wrong. That I misheard him or that there's some other alternative meaning behind his question.

"You're scared. Of the future to come, of failing. You told me you're not sure if you could do this. If you didn't need to be here, if this wasn't all part of some grand scheme and you had any choice, would you want this life?"

"But I don't have any of those choices. Even so, how could I go back to the life I lived before now even if I did want to?" I answer, a muffled plea to change the subject. Is it because you're unsure of the answer, or scared of what that answer is?

"Then humor me." Even if he is listening to my thoughts, to my pleas, he persists.

"I don't know. Yes... No..." My head turns to look at my feet, at the world below this rock instead of the one ahead. In the few short seconds of gathering my thoughts, I try to think of my answer. Before I can fully process, words begin to spill out. "I don't know. I wish I did. I wish I could say either yes or no and mean it. Yes I want this life. That there's nothing I would change and know in heart, mind, and soul that this is exactly where I am meant to be with certainty. But I also know how scared I am. How almost every fiber of my being is terrified all of the time of what's happened and what is still yet to come. I can't remember a time when I wasn't this scared, even before coming here." There's another pause between my words as they begin to come more easily. Not an answer to his question, but an answer nonetheless. "All I know is that, even in any choice or opportunity I may be given, I would never erase what I know now. I wouldn't want a memory where everything from this life that I've learned about and been through is gone completely. I wouldn't want to live a life where I didn't know you. Where I never got to discover who I am."

"And if you were still in your life from before, what would that look like right now? What would you want?"

"Again, I'm not sure. I can't really even remember what my life was like before. I didn't really have much of one to begin with, after the accident. I think some part of me always knew that the life I had before wasn't true. That there was something missing. Though, I guess that missing part became normal enough that I was able to ignore it. I don't want to ignore that part anymore. I think I used to imagine that one day I would ask Meg for a job at Mamma's, maybe one day opening my own diner. Perhaps graduating, going to college. Finding that whole white-picket fence life others always seem to go on about."

"You know, you say you don't know who you are yet, but I do. I know you, Serelia."

"And what do you know about me?" I bite my tongue awaiting his answer, unsure if I should be scared or not of his response.

"I guess it will be another answer you'll have to decode for yourself," he smirks as his gaze shifts ahead. "But I will tell you that I know you the same way I know it is you who is going to end this war."

"And if I don't? If I fail?"

"I'm willing to take every chance on you."

"Why? Why me?"

"Put it this way. If you ever did try to jump off of the cliff, I will be there to catch you. Always."

"Strangely, I don't doubt that for a second."

As his gaze keeps ahead, I follow his line of sight to see the sun beginning to peak above a mountain range that reveals itself with the morning light. Blues and pinks bleeding into the black of the night. The stars become replaced by clouds that stretch as wide as the forest. The water of the river is still streaming, a serene song with the notes of some chirping birds and the hoots of a lonesome owl.

Just like being between the two differing forests, night and day are broken by one another. One not fully present because of the other. It's probably only been a few hours since we've been here, time here feels nonexistent. We could have been up here forever, lifetimes passed, and I wouldn't have cared.

"I'm scared," the word breathes out of me before I can realize. "I'm scared of having to fight this monster when I can barely fight the one within me. The one inside of my head."

"I'm scared too," his reply surprises me and there's a wondering of what he means before he goes on. "I was terrified when your father ordered me to finally bring you here to the forest. When I thought you were going to die and I couldn't stop it. I'm afraid that all that is evil within these worlds will always expand until there is nothing left to fight for. Nothing good at least, nothing worth fighting for. What scares me most is that when the world comes to its end, it'll be because I failed."

"How do you deal with it? The fear." I almost beg the answer out of him, desperation lining with the words.

"I wish I knew. I try to remind myself that life isn't about running away or jumping off of the cliffs we come across. It's instead taking these moments to realize the beauty that awaits beyond them. Aside from that, I guess it's something we'll have to figure out together."

An airy sigh breaths out past my lips. Tiredness begins to fill my being, I slouch sideways. My shoulder presses against Caesar's arm, my head following as it leans against his shoulder. I allow myself to feel completely safe with him. "Can we start to figure it out tomorrow? Tonight, for a minute, I want to watch the sun rise without thinking of what is going to happen tomorrow." Without wondering how many tomorrows I have left. I want nothing more than to let this here be my world for as long as possible, where time is limitless and my nightmares can't follow me way up here. I send my silent wish up into the universe.

His body relaxes under my weight, his own head dropping so that it rests on mine. A matching sigh exhales out of his nose. "Whenever you're ready, Doll."

Chapter 19

Even as the sun begins to ascend behind the trees, the faint glow signifying a new day reminds me that I am nowhere near ready for what today will bring. Though I know time won't allow for us to remain up here forever and we need to head back to reality. If reality is what you can call this life.

Our journey back down is silent, aside from a brief comment here and there. Caesar walks the rest of the way with me until we reach Verena's cabin. Moving towards the front door, Caesar remains behind me until I enter, I hesitate to twist the brass knob. A worry brewing inside, fearful if my nightmares await me back inside.

"Serelia?" Caesar questions, his voice inches closer as the sound of a footstep follows his words.

"Everything's okay," my hand drops back down to my side and my head tilts upward in hopes to prepare myself for what's inside. "I'm fi- I'll be okay. I just needed a moment, but every-thing will be okay."

"You can say it as much as you want, we both know those words are further from the truth the more you try to make me believe them," he argues.

Biting down on my bottom lip, a heaveful sigh breathes out as my eyes briefly flutter close. "I'm scared to go back to sleep," I stumble through the words, unable to meet his gaze.

"I know," he says, though I stay silent. "Do you need... would you like me to come inside and stay with you for the remainder of the night?" His words stutter out as his eyes droop into a low, softened expression.

The word 'yes' burns against my tongue. I bite down, clenching my teeth on my tongue and swallowing the word before it could ever escape. "I'll be okay," my head drops knowing that I'm failing to convince either of us. "I don't know if I'll sleep, but I think I still need to process everything. To try and figure out how to be ready."

Turning back face to face with the door, this time I push it open and shove down any hesitancy or fear deep down. Settling back into my bedroom, plopping down onto the firm mattress, I struggle with the simple task of closing my eyes.

There is a comfort in knowing the real world is a world away, yet the reduction to a literal counting of sheep, or wolves in my case, is no help in what is inevitably becoming another sleepless night.

Time is not much of a concept here, no clocks hanging on anyway or sitting on any shelves to indicate how long it has been. I can only assume it's been mere minutes as the sun has not visibly moved any higher and I am still sitting here twiddling my thumbs to force my body to remain awake.

My brain skips over all of the events that have occurred in the span of the last few days, designing a list of all that is now real in my life. Forming bullets of everything that I have learned to be true, the legends and fairy tales that are so much more than stories. How they're now my entire life.

Soon enough, my list of what I now know as real becomes a list of what the next tomorrow will hold, and all that I fear that will come from it.

It isn't much longer until the sun fully mounts on its perch in the sky and I hear the knock of Verena's fist on my bedroom door.

Following a brief rhythm of thumps, the door pushes open with her stepping with it. As her eyes instantly land on me sitting up, my back against the headboard, there's a slight raise in her eyebrows. "The night did not treat you well, did it?"

"Trust me," my eyebrows mimic the movement of hers as my legs swing over the edge and I stand, "I feel worse than I look."

"I can absolutely assure you that the training you are about to endure will be of no help. In fact, it might worsen this whole zombied-out look you have going on," there's a glint behind her eyes as she pokes fun at me while she is already fully dressed and apparently eager for today's start. "You should hurry, I doubt you'll want extra laps for being late on your first day now.

I know wolves love the rush of a good run, but humans... not so much."

"I'll be ready in a minute," I say, flinging one of my bags onto the bed and taking out a simple workout set. Throwing my hair up into a quick bun, it's not even ten minutes later until I'm following Verena out onto the training grounds in the camp.

The closer we approach, my eyes draw onto Caesar standing beside Caiden next to one of the weapon racks. Whatever conversation he's engaged in stops as he notices me nearing, a slight smirk lifting on his lips. Verena goes on ahead of me, taking off with Caiden and leaving Caesar and me to train.

"You should have taken my offer to stay the night," he chimes out. "Perhaps then, I'd actually be able to see your eyes rather than the dark circles that have taken residence upon your face."

"The sun is barely waking up yet I'm here and actually dressed. You're lucky you got me to even walk here this early when I could still be in bed." I counter. His smirk remains plastered as he folds his arms over his chest. "Well?" He cocks his head as I silently inquire for him to say something, though his lips press closed, yet that smug simper never fades. "I thought we were here to train."

"Are you sure you wouldn't prefer to go back to bed? Wait until the sun wakes up." Despite the satirized nature that laces his voice, there's a glimpse of waiting behind Caesar's eyes. A waiting to see if I am truly ready for this. To not run or jump off the edges of the world, but rather try and discover the beauty the world holds beyond it. So that's exactly what I am going to do, even if the sun isn't awake.

I don't need to verbally respond for Caesar to notice my intent, uncrossing his arms and flicking his hand towards a rack with gleaming swords propped against the bars.

"I guess there's no beginner courses or any fighting for dummy starters here," my eyes focus on the blades as Caesar draws one of them off the rack, the sound of the honed weapon scraping against the metal of the bars. An oddly satisfying sound.

Caesar grips the hilt between his palm, the blade puncturing some unlucky air before his wrist drops and the steel drags along the dirt leaving a visible trail as it traces against the ground. His fingers tap against the metal, allowing for me to choose my own weapon.

"So us training with, I don't know, some sticks or maybe putting some saran wrap against the sharp bits is out of the question?" My eyes dance between the swords, studying the patterns and designs, each one unique. Each one telling its own story, the way Verena's axes tell hers.

Without any other thought, I seize one of the blades in front of me, the sword almost calling to me as the wooden hilt sheathed in juniper leather finds its way into my grasp. My arms nearly fall with the weight of the sword, but I force it back up so that the base is visible. The morning sun reflects off of the tip, highlighting the engravings on the sword to reveal they're not patterns like the others, but words. At least I think they're words from the way the script lines down the metal. My eyes continue down, seeing the way the sword rests easily in my hands, lining down until they reach the very end where a carmine ruby impresses in the silver beneath the grip.

Peering back onto the inscriptions incised onto the weapon, I try to imagine what it says, the ancient and foreign words almost speaking clear in my ears.

"Primis," Caesar breathes from behind me. "The first."

"First what?" I ask, my eyes still trained on the sword.

"The first alpha. That sword holds the legend of how the first leader, the first of us, came to be. Primis was the first true Lupi in this world. A warrior who battled against the Virunis to generate a new pack within the lands, one which held not only survival, but freedom. To ensure our abilities couldn't be used as a weapon for those with malicious intents of dominance in what they called fate. Primis was the first of us to fight, therefore, they were the first alpha." As I turn to face him, he grabs the sword from my grip, his finger tracing along the text. "There is no wondering why this sword spoke to you the way it did. Every Lupi has a weapon that is theirs, one that not only they choose, but chooses them in return. One that bonds with the soul of its possessor, that will call out to them despite any separation. Verena has her axes, your father with his bow, I have my sword," he hoists the lowered sword still in his clutch. The blade, one darker in its gray color compared to the silver one I have, with stars dispersed along the base alongside different letterings around—names. An obsidian marking the end of the weapon, a black and red stone that matches the colors of Caesar's eyes.

"So this is mine now?" He lifts the sword slightly to hand it back over and I take it back into my hold.

"Not exactly," he begins, leading me back onto the center of the training grounds. "Each weapon is unique to its keeper. This sword has existed long before any of our time, it is now here to remind us. Perhaps that is why today you were so drawn to its presence. But when the time comes for a weapon to bind with who you are, trust me, you'll feel it."

"So where do we begin today?" Lifting the heavy sword, I push it out at arms length and sway it around in a circular motion. This can't be right. It wobbles in my grip and it becomes a struggle to keep my arms up without dropping the sword completely.

"Here." He places his sword onto the ground and moves until he is back around me. Wrapping his arms around my own, he presses his hands near my wrists and adjusts my grip along the hilt before then controlling the motion in which the blade moves. The aroma of cinnamon and pine along with a hot breath beating against my neck sends a flutter across my skin, one that stretches all the day down to where his hands lie on my forearms, to my fingertips that envelop around the sword.

"With a sword, this is the most brutal type of fight you could face. One that never stops, always either on the defense or the attack. Where a hesitation could lead to your final falling." As we get into the momentum of swaying the sword around in front of us, his body then pushes against mine, forcing me to step forward as he impels my arms in the same direction ahead. "Always follow through with the sword. What you do, so will the blade. That is the only way you will remain in control. With each step, that gains the strength that will power each swing. And with each attack you strike, you must always be prepared for the countermove."

"Pointy end goes into the bad guy," my breath hitches as he forces us forward again in another jabbing motion. "Is there really so much thought process going on in a fight?"

"Not thoughts," he continues to swirl our arms together. I find myself lost and almost limp as I allow him to control the sword and me. "Instinct." Another heated breath prickles on my neck and there's a quick tremble in my knees. His hold around me tightens keeping me upright, the warmth of his body completely leans against my own. He twists our arms in a faster momentum, swinging the sword so that it now creates a whoosh of air to the invisible opponent ahead.

With his hand still firm against mine, I turn my head to face him behind me. His arms stop moving the sword altogether, but his clasp doesn't release, remaining secure around me. The breath I felt against my neck now beating against my face, his face only a mere inches away. The intensity of his eyes drilling into mine the way they did last night.

Seconds pass and Caesar's grip begins to loosen as he lets me begin swinging the sword on my own. Soon I can feel my arms steady with the flow of each movement, feeling the potent surges that rush through with each plunge. Repeating the same motion over and over again, I lose myself in the hypnotic oscillations of the blade. Caesar reaches down to grab his own sword from the ground before proceeding into a defensive stance in front of me.

"Come on," he lifts the sword up higher, urging me to make the first move.

The sword nearly drops as fast as my jaw at the thought of him swinging that weapon anywhere near me. "You want me to fight you? With these?" His eyes light up in amusement, a lifting furrow of his brows and an obvious bite of his own tongue to keep him from saying anything. Instead, he simply tips his head to the side, his sword following the same action, affirming for me to do the same. An anxious grunt rises from my chest mixed with an uneasy sigh as I imitate his stance. "Seriously, no sticks?"

"Plant your feet, keep your arms up," he says and pushes his sword forward. In one fell swoop almost entirely knocking my weapon from my fingertips. Their connection sends a loud and screeching echo of the metal clashing together.

"Hey!" Readjusting the hilt steady in my grip, Caesar doesn't give me a second to regain my stance before swinging again. Jumping back as the tip nearly grazes my abdomen, I yelp. "What the hell, I wasn't ready."

"And when there's other wolves attacking, or you get injured, are you supposed to call timeout in that moment to become settled?" His derisive question matches the merriment that flashes in his eyes. He steps in for another attacking move and I push my sword to deflect it. My legs strain to hold my position as his weight forces me back. "Step forward and swing through," he draws the sword towards him again, raising it over his head and casting it back down at me. In a swift shuffle, I intercept his blade that moves towards my neck. Leaning my body sideway, my feet follow as they shamble out of the sword's path and make an attacking move of my own. One which Caesar was able to track and escape with ease.

Continuing to go through different motions, the both of us swinging the swords in offensive and defensive attacks, I struggle to keep the momentum and gain any upper hand.

"Can I ask," I say while raising my sword and leaping forward to intersect him. "Just last night, Aryce told you that someone died. Someone from this pack. Someone that you all cared for, though I can't even tell because none of you have reacted to it to show it. I mean, you do care, don't you? Don't you feel anything?"

He stays quiet, his only response is a quick swipe of his sword.

"Lupi can't grieve the deaths of a warrior until the battle is won. Emotions can be a weakness, one that would prevent us from fighting or even surviving for as long as we have."

"You're still part human," I faintly protest. "Maybe it's pushing down your emotions that is causing these wars in the first place. I can't imagine living in any sort of world, magical or not, where I have to survive without being able to feel anything." I realize that pushing down emotions, finding any way to pry any hint of happiness, of sadness, or anything really, as far away as possible, is something that's not unfamiliar to me either. It's what I've been doing for years.

We keep training in silence, the only noise sounding from the clashes of the swords as they strike one another midair. Powering through each attack, my confidence slowly builds with each block, and I soon manage to lead Caesar's hands down and when his sword touches the ground, I kick the center which sends the blade flying from his grasp. Finally with the upperhand, I drive the sword ahead.

Before I can become enthused, or even believe, that I gained the advantage over Caesar, his fingers wrap around my wrist, locking me in place. As his hand halts me from moving any further and powerless to break free, his other hand snatches the sword from my clasp. There's not even a second between that and him kicking his leg around mine which causes me to drop, my back against the ground and him hovering over me and with the sword hanging where a single twitch can have it grazing my throat.

His eyes interlock with my own and I can see his mouth moving, but I can hear no words register as he speaks. A shadow strokes past behind his head, one that I can barely catch and follow in my limited view. It guides back to the same trees, the trees where I saw her.

"Caesar, she's back," I alert, my heart stopping as I watch the shadow form into a being.

Epilogue

His pupils bounce between my eyes, only a brief moment where I can see him soaking in the fear that overcomes me as I sense her presence. His head ever so slightly turns, his eyes trailing along trying to gather any sense of her being here, remaining subtle in his expressions, I can feel his body tense above me.

There's a tight clench in his jaw and I can see how the world around him evaporates as he focuses on the tree lines behind him, already knowing his next move but waiting for the perfect moment.

There's a shift in his body and his face turns fully behind him, and just as I think he's about to do something, he simply stands up, his sword lowered at his side.

What is he doing?

"Serelia," he continues to scan the camp around us, but his muscles relax and the teeth in his jaw release. "There's no one there."

"What?" A gasp forms in my throat as I repeat his motion and stand besides him, my eyes trained onto the tree line, the figure no longer there. "She's here, Caesar... She was here at least. I saw-" My voice dwindles, not finishing my sentence, as I turn my attention back to him.

"Your mind is trying to get the best of you, preying on your fears. Don't let it." There's a calming sincerity as he speaks, probably thinking this is because of my nightmares from last night. I'm about to say more when he goes on to reassure me. "We've doubled our guard and defenses since the last Crimson appearance here. We're on top of everything to make sure that she or any of her pack can not get past one of our wolves without us knowing about it. I promise you, Doll, you're safe here." He lifts his sword and takes a couple of steps back so that he is now opposite of me once more. "Come on," he motions for me to do the same. "We'll train for a bit longer before going in for breakfast."

I can't help but look at the tree line past his head, waiting for the shadow to reappear. I know what I saw. I know that this isn't some trick of the mind. There was something there.

My tongue glides against my upper teeth before biting down, an impulse in me wanting to do something. To go over there and see for myself. But I trust Caesar, he wouldn't lie to me or say something he didn't believe was true. Breaking contact with the shadows, my eyes land on the ground beneath me. Everything's okay, I try to convince myself. There's a punching in my gut that is shouting at me otherwise, I go to pick up my sword from the ground. As I draw the weapon back up, settling my fingers around the hilt, I look back at the tree line one more time just in case.

It's there.

Emerging from the deep umbra, the darkened figure reemerges, still a shadow hiding in shadows, but the figure of a human outline is clear as ever. My body numbs, freezing over completely, and before I can scream, or say anything, or even blink, the silhouette swoops from its position far away and a dark haze travels towards me, consuming any light within my sight. An intense burning radiates through my skull, the haze incinerating any last light.

A flare rages in my eyes, blistering them as if turning them to ash. I want to scream, to allow the sound to surround me. But the sweltering in my throat doesn't allow that one, desperate relief I crave. Instead it is stuck in that void between my brain and vocal chords.

The flare ignites into a flame, a flash of light across darkened sights. The flashes pulsing between pure light and dark until there is nothing but light. The pain becomes so intense I begin to feel detached from my own body. Yet that is something too good to even wish for as the agony jolts across me. Every sense within begging for me to succumb to the pain, yet one by one those senses are cremated by the burning that only continues to grow hotter.

Then the light dims. The burning begins to cool. The pain softens to mere aching.

Then the fire becomes an explosion.

My vision goes red. Crimson red.

The pain I thought I felt before being nothing to the one that absorbs me now. There's nothing but pain and red. Losing consciousness, her voice vibrates in my head, keeping me alive.

Pain lasts seconds. The future is the only guarantee.

In the red, images begin to crystalize.

A wolf. Red eyes. White fur. Red and black smoke spreads across a scorching sky. Tick, tick, tick, a clock spins backwards and time reverses. A dagger pierces into flesh. Blood seeps into dirt. Its light sprinkle strengthens into a storm of blood, raining down until the soil stains red. Bodies float through a sea of blood. Weapons drifting besides them. A beating heart thumping, thumping, thumping. At least until it dies. Wolves. So many dead wolves.

The scorching within expels to the outside. The metal of the sword heats under my fingertips. Every sense my body possesses surcharges, an overwhelming that tires my frail being. My body becomes engulfed by each whisper of the wolves, the gust of wind that floods my ears, the steel of the sword in my palms, the sharp scent of the dew of wet grass, the metallic blood that trickles down my tongue and along my teeth. The stinging of a sharp itch spreads within my gut, my chest. Sharp claws scratch against my skin, the wolf that resides somewhere inside fighting to break free. These visions give it the power to resist whatever holds it inside. But I have no control.

The white wolf returns. Then there's another. A brown wolf. Golden eyes sparkling opposite of the white wolf's red. A sword falls from the stars. A million stars that glisten upon a blackened canvas. The blade strikes into the space between the two wolves. Uno morsu rubeus regnabit etched into the metal. The silhouettes of faceless beings distend along every tree in the surrounding forest. Their breaths form a thick fog through the air. One that rises high until the stars are no longer visible. Then they vanish. The two wolves are all that are remaining. Wait, no. There's one more. One more wolf that is still hiding in the shadows.

The blade brands itself into my flesh. Through the pain, the sword wills me to stand. My body lulls itself towards Caesar. In the brief flickers between the visions and I can see him, he dodges my attacks. A hiss stinging from his mouth as our blades collide. Any attempt I make to draw my arms away from him ends with my body pulling it back down. Harder, faster. Smarter against each move he makes. Something within was willing me to kill him. That I wouldn't stop until I did.

Stop. I need to stop. Why am I doing this? Why is she making me do this?

Nothing in my mind can process as the visions persist. Another seeps into my mind to block out any voice I have left. The flickers of reality blending until all I see is what she wants me to see.

A war of wolves. Or the end of one. Skeletons buried into the forest grounds. Blood drenching the fur of so many fallen Lupi. Me, kneeling in a land I've never seen. Hands, I think mine, dropping with the thick, red liquid. The shadow of a single wolf stretching over the piles of corpses, stretching over everything dead and gone. A single golden light flickering amidst the shadows. Rain pouring down, no longer a storm of blood, but of tears. Up until the golden light goes out.

The flames in my vision grow cold. The red that stretches across my sight dulls until the sun's light can finally pierce through. The claws remove their hold on my insides, no longer trying to break free. I regain control of my body, which instantly falls from the remaining suffering still afflicting me, though it continues to fade. My surroundings clear and find Caesar kneeling down in front of me.

When inhaling to breathe out a sigh of relief, solace that the pain is gone, one final burning flames across my body and the air sucks harshly into my lungs. These burns are more concentrated, running across my bare arms. No, not my arms. My scars, the ones from the accident. Stinging as if I am being cut all over again from the shards of glass. An even more painful reminder, one that they wanted me to feel.

One final blow of the pain agonizes as the world all too quickly surrounds me again. Her grasp finally releases its hold over me. A sobbing scream rings in my ears. A scream that strains every nerve and tears at the thin flesh in my throat as it frees itself. I realize that it's my scream that rings in my ears. A scream that strains every nerve and tears at the thin flesh in my throat as it frees itself. My fingers dig into the ground beneath, a warm liquid spilling as I pierce the ground.

My breathing eventually slows. The last of my screams belting out until my throat is completely raw. Caesar hovers above still, his face etched with panic. A heaviness keeps my head against the ground, only able to see what's right ahead of me. As my body struggles to recover, I take note of the blueness of the sky. The white clouds shaped across the vivid cyan. Caesar's hands scramble in front of him and I can feel him pry my fingers from the floor, drawing them up in his own. A dark fluid soaking my fingertips.

His head turns, scanning my body for injury until he reaches my face. His eyes find mine. His mouth moves to speak, but the ringing blocks out any sound of his voice. Yet the words "I'm sorry" that shape upon his lips are not hard to recognize, his eyes saying the exact same.

Still numbed from her control, I don't bother to try to move. Instead, my vision blurs, a wet heat streaking down my face. How much more of this pain will I need to endure? How will I survive this pain? Or worse? With his free hand, Caesar wipes the falling tears.

A large part of me wants to yield to the lasting pain. All of the flames and burning have died, yet there is a lasting impression within me that I'm not sure will recover anytime soon, if ever. An impression that wants to forever elude any more pain to come. Holding a desire to be buried where I currently lie, knowing that I did try but lost.

But I can't.

I need to hold on to the fact that there is so much more at stake than the few seconds of pain I will endure. With everything Caesar said to me in the forest last night, his belief in me, how can I let him down? Let everyone down.

I can't let myself down.

That starts with me getting back up.